Enter a Dragon —
Stage Centre

Enter a Dragon —
Stage Centre

An Embroidered Life of Mrs Siddons

CARYL BRAHMS

HODDER AND STOUGHTON
LONDON SYDNEY AUCKLAND TORONTO

British Library Cataloguing in Publication Data
Brahms, Caryl
Enter a dragon—stage centre
I. Title
823'9'1F   PR6001.B6E/

ISBN 0-340-22377-4

Dedication

For Veronica Silver who gave me the print of Mrs Siddons which for a time belonged to our dear Nora Nicholson and which now hangs on my wall in a pose which precludes her from eying me accusingly.

Acknowledgments

My grateful thanks to Mr Rivers Scott at Hodder and Stoughton who has been a model of patience with me, and of optimism and helpfulness:

Also

To the Head Librarian and Staff of the London Library and in particular to Mr Matthews to whom I must have been a great trial but who never even raised an eyebrow.

BOOK ONE
"Drat the Girl"
Eighteenth Century Gallery-Goer

⊰ Chapter 1 ⊱

THE parchment in the centre of the bow window of the Chymist's shop at Hockley-in-the-Hole was old and faded for it had served as harbinger in many a straggle of village and neat, self-respecting country town. But to the thin boy, all wrists and chilblains, in the crooked steel-rimmed spectacles, it was part of the magic that was to hold him in lifelong thrall.

February 15th, 1755, it was headed. The boy examined it carefully so that not a word, not a crooked letter, should escape him, as became a future Drama Critic and theatrical biographer:

MR KEMBLE'S COMPANY OF COMEDIANS

At the Barn in Farmer Broadribb's Yard This
Evening will be Performed A CONCERT OF MUSIC
(to begin at exactly 6 o'clock).

*

Tickets to be obtained by the purchase of
one pot of the new London TOOTH-PASTE

*

Between the Parts of the Concert will be
Presented, GRATIS, a Celebrated Historical Play
(Never Before Presented Here)

HAMLET,

PRINCE of DENMARK

The Characters to be Dressed in Ancient
Habits, according to the Fashion of those Times.
To which shall be added a Comedy

THE MINOR

There followed the cast list and a truly remarkable N.B.—

The DOG that so Distressed our LADY PATRONS
on our last Visit to this temporary
Temple of the Arts will be securely
tethered in the Barn opposite.

* * *

In spite of the east wind with its spicing of ice the boy glowed.
He made towards the door of the shop and fumbled at the latch.
Enthusiasm had set his spectacles a little more askew.

At the counter a large woman, like a perambulating tent, was
counting out a batch of tickets with Mr Fazackerley, the Chymist.
She was Betsy Noakes, Nannie to the present infant Kemble
and several subsequent infant Kembles, not forgetting general
smacker of bottoms to the ragtag and bobtail of brats who
tagged along with the company and were in need of such salutary

attention; she was also ticket-taker, prompter and "Court Lady", "Crowd", and candle-snuffer.

"Fifty-six and one on the nod," she announced, "and that's all the barn will hold with comfort, what with the set-up stage and Madam Kemble's bassinet. And Mr Kemble's compliments to Mr Fazackerley," the perambulating tent reminded herself, "and would you kindly oblige with a mortar and pestle for the Apothecary."

"In *Hamlet*?" questioned the Chymist mildly.

"*Romeo*—if requested."

Mr Fazackerley obliged. "There now," said the making-ready-to-depart black tent, "that's nice as ninepence. Shakespeare!" she attributed with brazen certainty.

"Really?" said the Chymist. He sounded doubtful. The boy in the crooked spectacles felt doubtful, too. He must remember to look it up. The kindly Chymist was now free to attend to the needs of his next customer.

"What can I do for you, young Sir?"

The boy blinked up at him.

"Please, Sir, how much is a tick . . . I mean a pot of London tooth-paste?" He held his breath.

"Three pennies," said the inexorable Mr Fazackerley. The boy peered panic-stricken into his purse. Suppose he had not enough money? He had not. His lips quivered.

"But I'll tell you what," said the Chymist, a dedicated follower of the Drama himself, instantly understanding all. "Nod or not, I shall have to arm Mrs Fazackerley from her party of Loo in town. If you care to saunter over around nine o'clock, you may slip into my seat for what remains of the spectacle— free."

The boy beamed and beetled off, bumping against the horse-post in his excitement; and such was his ecstasy that he did not even stop to rub his elbow. Tonight, he promised himself, at nine—say half-past eight—in case.

Now it so happened that nine p.m. at Farmer Broadribb's Barn was near panic-time for Gertrude, Queen of Denmark, who, in her proper personage of Madam Kemble, was to bring up a family of future Belvideras and Jaffiers, at suitable intervals, on the Brecon-to-Bristol stroller's circuit. The night, as in the words of the Bard, had been unruly—and that was an understatement of Shakespeare's. It had started, so to say, after luncheon, had there been any, which there had not, unless you counted Farmer Broadribb's field of raw turnips on which the little troupe had illicitly fallen. Since when matters had gone from appalling to even worse.

The Infant (one sensed the capitals; clearly they aggrandised her above the bobtail rabble of brats of lesser members of the troupe, and so they did, at least in the mind of the Guv'nor's Lady, Madam Kemble). The Infant, then, had fallen into a fretfulness, and not a first tooth in sight! This fretfulness was communicated to Betsy Noakes, causing her habitually apple-red cheeks to turn an unbecoming purple and impelling her to throw the company broom at offenders instead of sweeping the barn with it. All Betsy's swans had turned out to be geese, it seemed, this dratted day—with the shining exception of Mr Fazackerley, the Chymist—and all her ribbon bows had turned into insoluble knots at the end of pigtails when tugged by small impatient fists and offered to her rheumaticky fingers to deal with. "There, there, there," she cooed, rocking the bassinet in a professionally soothing manner, "there, there, there," but her face looked menacing to those who could read the signs.

Then the set-up stage refused to allow itself to be, as it were, set up, but half subsided into a tilt, like Richard the Third's hump-backed shoulder. Then, too, there had been the inexplicably unsteady return of Mr Kemble from his courtesy call on the Mayor of Hockley-in-the-Hole, at His Honour's Parlour. Had she not known him to be a model of sobriety despite his Profession, Gertrude, Queen of Denmark, would have sworn her husband was The Worse, so little communion did his noble head appear to hold with his legs.

The arrival of an audience of mainly drunken farmers and butchers from miles around, with their merry wives (all that mulled Negus, thought Gertrude, Queen of Denmark, darkly) with a raucous fringe of yokels, did nothing to improve matters. One yokel in particular had proved very tiresome indeed. He had turned from baiting Farmer Broadribb's chained-up dog and presented himself at the doors of the temporary Temple of Thespis without a ticket and without so much as a pot of London tooth-paste, claiming not to be aware of the customary Polite Pretence—it was the same every autumn and Madam Kemble was fair tired of the prank. He knew as well as anyone present—and a little crowd of yokel yahoos was now collecting —that there were two kinds of Theatrical Spectacles: those presented in the Patent Theatres, and those presented in the pomping halls, barns and inn-yards, unlicensed by the Lord Chamberlain's office, which, therefore, were forced to be per- formed by subterfuge, such as proclaiming themselves concerts for which, as we have seen, tickets would be "given away" with a pot of London tooth-paste. Not that the travelling troupes had not their proper pride, in spite of their designation—handed down from the days of Elizabeth of England—of Rogues and Vagabonds, a label they resented deeply.

"We are Thespians," Gertrude, Queen of Denmark, addressed herself to the gaping crowd. "Thespians," she repeated with icy clarity. "Why, even the great Garrick himself would rejoice to act Richard the Third in the Dog Days, before the hottest kitchen fire, for a sop in the pan as Samuel Foote puts it; and so would I," she added under her breath. She never would advise or encourage any persons to make themselves voluntary vagabonds.

Then there was going to be trouble with the Lord Hamlet. It had been Strolling Practice, ever since the days of Grand

Old Burbage himself, to divide takings among the histrionic brotherhood into twenty-four shares. Six parts went to the Management as Actor-Manager, and one each to the rest of the players and to those of the Guv'nor's family who were taking part in the performance. But this was not all. As the only provider of scenes and costumes, the Guv'nor was entitled by honoured custom to four more parts. At the end of each performance the players assembled for an accounting. After sundry deductions for a mysterious stock debt which, however often it was reckoned, never seemed to decrease, and the routine costs for candles, paper and ale, the pitiful remainder was shared out among them. The Lord Hamlet knew this as well as he knew the number of fingers on his hand. Yet he pouted when awarded the glorious total of eighteen pence and two candle ends. Who did he think he was – Wee Davy? This boded no good for this evening's performance, Madam Kemble confided to their stentoriously snoring Manager, Mr Kemble. Could it be that her honoured spouse was sleeping it off? Madam Kemble banished the thought as unworthy of her.

By the time our young playgoer had inserted himself into the seat vacated by his friend Mr Fazackerley the Chymist, the paying patrons had steamed themselves into an ugly mood. They had jeered all through the concert kindly provided by members of the cast, who by now had embarked upon a much-cut version of *Hamlet* and arrived in some sort of order at the play scene to boos and catcalls. But at this point Gertrude, Queen of Denmark, showed her true mettle by sailing forward and announcing that the Lord Hamlet would now delight the Court with a Hornpipe. She looked confidently at the Lord Hamlet who was never known to be loath to show off. But the Lord Hamlet, though he could hear the cue perfectly well, was studying his nails almost as though they had been clean. Gertrude, Queen of Denmark, tried again: "Will delight the Court with a Hornpipe," she announced with great clarity. By now one could have heard the yokels' sucked straws drop. But the Lord Hamlet had turned his attention to his side-curls. He patted them. It was a pity they were so dusty. "A Hornpipe," said Gertrude, Queen of Denmark, at her most magisterial. Sullenly, since the House was all for a jig, the Lord Hamlet complied.

Our young playgoer did not join in the general applause. He had read the play as became a future Drama Critic right through the tooth-ache that had kept him from school and he was fairly sure that the author had made no mention of a Hornpipe at this point. Possibly just before Hamlet was shipwrecked on his way to England—they were all mad there—he reminded himself fair-mindedly.

The Drama concluded, the paying patrons stood not upon the order of their going but stumbled out of the rushlight and candleshine of the barn into the wet and chill and darkness of the night, leaving the famished company of Barnstormers to cluster round their manager, a pack of financial vultures, intent on his not bubbling them as he had at Moreton-in-the-Marsh. The young unpaying patron, loath to forsake the neighbourhood of Magic, was left alone with Madam Kemble's bassinet and its contents. Gaze met gaze, and for a time neither faltered. Finally, the contents of the bassinet outgazed the future James Boaden.

"Gug," said the future Sarah Siddons.

⊰ Chapter 2 ⊱

THE pompers were pomping. Six years had passed without making any noticeable difference to their draggletail routine—nor to their restive audiences. Roger Kemble's dauntless troupe were still strolling—what else, indeed, give a shabby, gesticulating Romeo, lose a shabby, gesticulating Shylock. But little Miss Kemble was now a mature six years of age and could clamber from Betsy Noakes' wheelbarrow, which she now had to share with her brother, John Philip, at the outskirts of the town and proceed in procession on her own two feet, bearing the drum on her head, as the Countess of Durham had done before her. "It is an Omen," Madam Kemble proclaimed. "It keeps the rain off," the more practical Betsy Noakes approved. The day would come when Sarah Siddons would ascribe the noble carriage of her head and the Queenly manner in which she wore a crown to her early training in bearing the pomping drum. But for the time being the smudge-cheeked cupid had turned drummer.

This week the strolling players were lucky. They were to join a travelling fair on the outskirts of Chipping Norton. There were many advantages to itinerant troupes picking up fairs on their strollings. Fairing folk were on the whole easy come, easy go vagabonds and with reasonable luck could offer a small tent or wooden booth to the Thespians. Then there were almost certain to be over-spills of merry-makers, happy to rest their feet or backs or both, or too full of ale, or for any or all of those reasons, happy enough to plump themselves down on stool or bench. But no matter how small the tent or stinking with the sweat of patrons long-departed the booth, the ceremonial parade of the players upon arrival at a town was never abandoned.

The straggle of strollers and their brats marched in tarnished tinsel and threadbare velvet to the beating of the proud drum along the main thoroughfare to the Mayor's Parlour or market square. "Tup'ny salad! Who'll buy my tup'ny salad?" called small Sarah. She thrust it at a rich-looking farmer's wife, there to sell her fine fresh garden cabbages, who could see at a glance that it was mainly composed of pesky dandelion leaves, and thrust it back.

"*Who'll* buy my tup'ny salad?" The future Mrs Siddons' pipe had crescended into a wail. But there were no takers. The Guv'nor stopped, gold-topped stick twirling, snuff-box at the ready, lacy handkerchief, though grubby, flourishing to left and right, to request leave to present the evening's Magic, which permission would be granted at the drop of a collecting-box. The pomping folk had come to town.

Today, a spitting, spattering kind of day, small Sarah, having relinquished her drum to Zekial Squob—who not only beat it but played both Gobbos by a magical change of hat with practised dexterity and his own carroty hair—small Sarah covered her corkscrew curls and their nearly-new ribbons with a framed daub of The Old Homestead due to be clutched by Black-eyed Susan, along with her innocent Bastard, on the snowy night she was turned out of it.

[17]

"What is a bastard?" Sarah enquired of her wheelbarrow-pushing Nurse, for Brother John Philip was still in it.

"You wicked little girl, just you wash your mouth out with soap!" said the scandalised Betsy, which, though it was unlikely, soap being the price it was, was not enlightening.

Dragging along near the tail of the defiant little procession trudged two little girls, bosom-friends if mud-bespattered.

" 'Tis not fair," said Kezia Quicktobed, the shorter, stockier of the two, "that Sairey has been given the picture to keep the rain off her ribbons." She tossed her dripping own.

" 'Tis never fair," agreed Salubria Golightly, the taller, blonder and, on the whole, cleaner of the pair.

"Stuck-up thing," said Kezia.

"Pride goes before a fall," prophesied Salubria.

"Prig," said Kezia.

"Show-off," they agreed.

Useless to deny that two pink tongues were put out in the direction of the happily unconscious future Sarah Siddons, sheltering under The Old Homestead, while the tattered tinsel of her dress took the brunt. Poor little Miss Kemble—of course she was a show-off. "Now then, Sairey, showing off again," Betsy Noakes was wont to say. "Not that you can help it, poor little mite, not with that example in front of your blessed eyes before they were rightly opened, showing-off being in your blood." And at this point Betsy would look balefully across the barn at Lady Macbeth in her proper person of Madam Kemble. "Poor innocent little lamb!"

"What does innocent mean—please?" asked the little lamb. Betsy, at a loss for any other answer, downed her charge's freshly laundered drawers and spanked her. "That'll learn Sairey to know turtles from jays! Shakespeare," she assured herself.

The next day was to be Fairings Day. Any lagging lion or recalcitrant caravan would have arrived by then. It was also to be a Benefit Night for Katherine-Queen-of-England-come-into-the-Court, for this was the role that Madam Kemble herself was to undertake, on which occasion little Miss Kemble, a fledgling Thespian, was to be led to the rushlights by her Mama, hopefully to be recognised by all and sundry as the Infant Prodigy that undoubtedly she was.

The great day dawned. Small Sarah had done her damnedest to go into a perilous calm immediately after breakfast (a windfall apple bruised only on one side and therefore eatable when chewed around) as she had so often seen her Mama do—and which her Mama had so often seen her sainted Mama do. Sainted? Well, sup or leave a mug of gin, and who could blame her in a life such as she led? Little Miss Kemble disposed of her calm thus early in the morning for fear her knees should knock while she waited in the Sides for her cue, so spoiling the effect of the commanding gesture with which Queen Katherine was to summon her to enter.

It was not that Madam Kemble had omitted to instruct her daughter with that same particularly clear speech that her own sainted Mama (well, Mama, at least, was accurate) had done before her. Sarah had barn-storming blood in her veins. Had she not been carried on anonymously but in Titania's own arms at the tender age of eighteen months? And had she not toddled stoutly on by herself as the young Prince Arthur in *King John* ("Oh, Hubert, not mine eyes!"), having fought and downed small Miss Salubria Golightly whose role this officially was—Nanny Noakes being too constricted by the many heavy flannel under-garments she insisted on wearing for her "Attendant Nymph" to prevent her in time. Sarah, born to the boards, was not one whit put out by a long rip in her freshly-laundered pantaloons and her wreath knocked awry. Had she not, indeed, been carefully coached into the most effective positions from which to declaim? Had not her balance been strengthened and stiffened by a mother's caring tuition? Madam Kemble, who had ever put Respectability before Art, upheld a standard of excellence before the eyes of her husband's troupe, a standard from which she would never depart, least of all with her own progeny, jeer though their public might—and jeer they did. It was by no means all bread and circuses at the Chipping Norton Goose Fair.

Seedy though the Acrobats, the Conjurers, the Barebacked Riders and the Tight-rope Walkers who travelled with the Fair might be, the pride of the *haute école* was in their bearing, for neither then nor now could circus folk hope to survive without its indispensable schooling. The excitement of seeing the handsome Lion-Tamer actually in the same cage as the old, shaggy and undoubtedly toothless Wild Creature in Captivity, however sleepy, and the warm gales of laughter called forth by the antics of the Joey and the Harlequins, not forgetting the poignant loss of yokel hearts to the plump and heavily-painted, if elderly, Columbine, ill-accorded with an appetite for Henry-the-How-Manyeth and his Six Wives, the dirty old man. Bluff King Hal was going to have his work cut out to hold his Public this Saturday night.

Awaiting Mama's dread summons in the Sides, the future Sarah Siddons, hearing the catcalls, bit her trembling lower lip right through.

The Sides: they acted as scenic wings on which were suspended long strips of paper with speeches and cues written out on them. In later life it became Sarah and John Philip's boast that they could memorise the Sides in forty minutes: indeed, at more mature ages than six and four respectively they actually embarked upon the tragedy of *Pizzaro* before Mr Sheridan had finished the last act. But at Time the Present Miss Kemble was standing voiceless and shivering in the Sides, while a cacophony of sound symbolising dissatisfaction arose in a raucous crescendo which abashed her terrified ears. But here Madam Kemble showed her true mettle as many a Mother to an Infant Prodigy has done both before her and since. With an imperious gesture she parted the crowd. It was composed in the main of Betsy Noakes, Zekial Squob, his wife and son-in-law, Zenobia Quick-tobed and her daughter Kezia, Peg Golightly and her daughter Salubria, Inigo Dankworth, pale-green with collywobbles, and his wife, Cleopatra Laine (clearly Inigo had worn himself to shreds playing the pipe and tabor to perfection), My Lord Hamlet, and Iacob Iacoby, the singing clown and Melancholy Iacques. Madam Kemble sailed into the Sides where she took her little daughter by the hand and intoned awfully:

"Do I quake?"

"No, Mama."

"Do I hang back when my Public calls?"

"No, Mama."

"Very well then."

And without further ado Katherine, Queen of England, led her Infant Prodigy out and propelled her down-stage to face the rushlights after the manner of a very tall ship pulling a very small tug in her wake; whereupon the din redoubled. The riotous fairgoers were in no mood to be fobbed off with an Infant Thingammy.

"Serves her right," mouthed Kezia Quicktobed to her bosom friend, Salubria.

"So it does!" mouthed Salubria Golightly back.

"Show-off," they rhubarbed.

"And now, daughter, Declaim!"

The saucer-eyed Sarah felt turned into stone.

"Think of Papa." Mama pointed to the Merry Monarch who, it so chanced, was looking exceedingly glum. "Think of Mama." Queen Katherine laid a heavily beringed and only slightly grubby hand on her heaving bosom. "Think," she exhorted, "of your Sainted Grandmama."

Anything was better than that.

Miss Kemble burst into the Nursery fable of the Frog who would a-wooing go.

From her place in the Trial Scene, Betsy Noakes mouthed the lines after her charge. They finished almost together and in triumph, and if not to the delight of all present, at least to their toleration.

The future Sarah Siddons had become a professional actress.

At the back of the barn a lean, long-legged boy with his steel-rimmed spectacles crooked, his face spotted as a pudding, had been all-attention through the frog's strange incantation. Thanks to a lucky aunt in the country and an attack of measles from which to convalesce, James Boaden had not missed a syllable of Sarah's début. Earlier in the evening, by dint of the time-honoured device of wriggling under the tent, he had witnessed the hair-raising ascent of Monsieur Lumière's balloon. But the Drama had exerted its usual charm for him and although he himself preferred the more classically pure refrain of Tippety-Wichet to that of the romantically inclined frog, at least it had furnished him with one of the theatrical events of his life.

For as he took his reluctant leave of the Magic O, as the Bard had defined it, with one last dazed look at it over his skinny shoulder, he bumped into a costume-carrying Madam Kemble and her cannon-pulling husband. The impact of Roger Kemble's boot against James Boaden's behind caused the boy to stagger into Katherine, Queen of England. He stood there wretched, rubbing and blinking.

"Young man," said Madam Kemble, "do you realise that you have just been kicked by one accounted the most Gentlemanly Falstaff in all England?"

What did a bruised behind matter measured against the most

Gentlemanly Sir John in England to a future Biographer and Drama Critic? James Boaden beamed. He started the long trudge back to Aunt Juniper's cottage with stars in his eyes, stars that never quite departed from them.

⊰ Chapter 3 ⊱

SIX more years passed, and the arrival of the Kembles in
town differed in some respects from the kind of Strolling of
the other Strollers. For one thing, Roger Kemble, though
by no means a rich actor-manager, could now afford an ancient
horse, Dapple, a left-over from a circus waggon, the better to
travel his wife, family and effects. It was Race Week in Worcester
—a meeting much sought after among Strolling Thespians. On
the Saturday night Miss Kemble, aged twelve, gave her Son of
Isabella in Southern's tragedy, *The Fatal Marriage or The
Innocent Adultery* in which the little boy turns to his Mama (and
there is no award for any reader guessing that Madam Kemble
was enacting the widow-presumptive):

> *Child:* Have you done a Fault? You cry as though you had . . .
> If you kiss me and look so very sad upon me, I shall
> cry too.

Most affecting the Company found it.

It is worthy of note that a Mr William Siddons was now on the playbill in the window of the most fashionable Chymist's — where else would the follower of the Drama expect to buy the new London tooth-paste with a ticket for a "Concert" tucked away?

In his new-found affluence Roger Kemble could lodge his fast-increasing family at an Inn, not only when his lady was giving birth and suckling, but whenever such accommodation could be acquired, so it was farewell, a not particularly fond farewell, to all those haystacks for the respectable Kembles.

None the less, partly in honest perplexity and partly from sheer habit, when some member of his Company asked him for a rise he would say: "Yes, I am an M.P. — Manager of a Playhouse: Mighty Poor: Much Plagued: More Puzzled how to pay your salary."

As late as 1776, as Tate Wilkinson has set it down, a Stroller could earn as little as thirteen shillings a week. Fortunately he could lodge at a humble Inn with board for four shillings a week, and so could afford to ignore the raw turnips which grew in the fields by the roadside, the staple diet of many a Stroller. Moreover, Tate Wilkinson, at one time an actor himself, left us a piteous description of some poor actress: "What was truly dreadful," he wrote, "was the draggle-tailed Andromache in frost, rain, hail and snow, delivering her Benefit Bills from door to door." At least our Sarah was to be spared this humiliation.

Tate Wilkinson was to prove a good friend to Sarah Siddons long before her redoubtable days, when he was to say of her, "There goes a lamp not to be extinguished, kept burning by unquenchable flame of soul."

The day being a Sunday, a fine Sunday, and a fine Sunday in high summer, found Madam Kemble attired in Isabella's sable weeds (*The Innocent Adultery*) negotiating the steps of the waggon.

[25]

Behind her Betsy, who had raided the costume hamper and borrowed the Nurse's garments from *Romeo and Juliet* to mark the importance of the occasion, huffed and puffed and wheezed herself up the stairs, assisted by Tom King, pushing from behind. It was to be a long haul before Tom would win his place in Garrick's company at Drury Lane. For the time being he accounted himself in luck to be offered Autolycus, one of the two Dromios and "a Responsible". In between barns he drove Dapple, to whom he was devoted. It took the weight off his feet. At Drury Lane he was to offer a snuff-box and flourish a plumed hat with the best of them, having watched Roger Kemble closely for some seasons; but now it was "Gee up" and the kindly crack of a whip nowhere near Dapple. Last, on this sunny Sunday came Sarah, skipping up the steps of the waggon in her new pink dress and ribbons, and such was her pleasure to be wearing it that she clean forgot to go into one of her perilous calms, for this was a summer day of summer days and on it the future Sarah Siddons was to be presented to her, hopefully, new school, an establishment on the outskirts of the town for the education of the Daughters of Gentlemen. Old Dapple, a straw hat (*As You Like It*) poised jauntily between his ears, clattered over the cobbles at less than break-neck speed. Tom King flicked his whip again, not at his dear old Dapple, but at some irresponsible passing fly; missed it, and shook a sombre head after it. Betsy nodded off.

Sarah's new pink dress deserves a pause in Dapple's progress to Thornloe House. When, flushed with success and exhaustion, Sarah begged her Mama to allow her to wear the new pink dress and ribbons, unsuitable though they were for the occasion, Madam Kemble had not the heart to refuse the child. After all the pretty ribbons and flounces could not fail to captivate the no doubt formidable Headmistress' heart.

"I do not know what her Sainted Grandmama would say!" she confided to her husband who had a pretty clear idea of what word his Sainted Ma-in-law—well, his Ma-in-law—might have hit on in her cups. A clap of thunder, as if it were her Sainted Mama's heavenly reaction to her son-in-law, recalled Madam Kemble to her senses. "You may wear it, daughter, if the weather holds, but not," she warned, "if it rains." On going to bed, Sarah took with her a Prayer Book, opened, as she sleepily supposed, at the prayer for fine weather, for the new pink dress, as she could not but be aware, suited her exceedingly. Soon she fell asleep, the book folded in her thin little arms. At day-break she awoke to find that she had been holding the prayer for rain to her budding bosom and that rain was streaming down the window. So Sarah went back to bed with the Prayer Book opened at the right place and when she awoke again she found her mistake quite remedied: for, as she was fond of recounting when she was an old lady, the sky was as pink and beautiful as the dress she was to wear.

"Someone looks like a sarsaparilla jelly," said Salubria, smoothing her own church-going sky-blue satin dress with the darns; almost they did not show.

Kezia smoothed her own, her puce dimity. "Frills is childish," she consoled herself.

"Show-off," not for the first time and certainly not for the last, they summed Sarah up.

At last Dapple came to a stop before a commodious house with a brass plate blazoning the information that Thornloe House was an establishment for the Education of the Daughters of Gentlemen. Headmistress: Mrs Hermione Worthington, College of Preceptors.

The equipage decanted itself. Three figures progressed up the drive. Betsy Noakes pulled the heavy front door bell.

They were shown into a smallish book-filled room—the Headmistress' study. From behind a large desk, full of silver-framed portraits of departed Head Girlies, the Headmistress arose:

"Madam Kemble? Ah, quite so. And this is?"

"Betsy Noakes, General Nurse," said Betsy, and made a curtsy so deep that it well-nigh unbalanced her.

"And this is little—ah—Susan, then?" A sweeping gesture paused at its summit to take in the pink-faced, pink-gowned Sarah.

"Pray," the Headmistress inclined a gracious head, "be seated."

Madam Kemble took the upright cane chair, specially placed there for culprits. It was hard on the female frame. Betsy plumped for the rocking chair—Mrs Hermione Worthington's own chair to which she would resort at more intimate moments, when chatting to Miss Melpomene Robinson, Mistress of the Globes.

And pink little Miss Kemble? At an age when she might have been forgiven for placing her weight first on her right foot, then on her left and wriggling somewhere in between, she stood erect, her head held high as though wearing some unseen Queenly crown, proud as a peacock.

"News has come to me of the high standard of both the conduct and the acting of your company."

"It is indeed good of you to see us on a Sunday—the only day we have free from moving on. Though what my Sainted Mama would say . . ."

For all her rosy apple-cheeks, Betsy Noakes shook a saddened head. Such Godless carryings on were not in the Holy Readings.

But the Headmistress was smiling benignly:

"One understands that the Demands of Art are indeed Imperious."

"I would have cut The Vale of Evesham," said Madam Kemble. "Gladly," she added with some truth. "And called on you tomorrow. But one's Public . . ."

"I understand. I myself have a handsome daughter of about your Susan's age. My Pamela shows quite a talent for Histrionics in the School play. Why, only last term, when Augusta Coldwell, our Head Girlie, fell out of the Leading Role, my Pamela stepped in at the last moment and acquitted herself admirably; quite the little professional."

"The Spectacle must go on," added Madam Kemble.

"And so I thought that—run away, little Susan and play with your new school-fellows—I thought that in exchange for the imparting to sweet Pamela of some acting skills, Thornloe House could take your dear Childie without payment. It would look so well in our School play programmes."

Madam Kemble fetched a deep sigh—the Lady in her sleep-walking scene could not have heaved a heavier. Respectability and Art were fighting in her bosom. It was a dead heat.

"Do not put your daughter on the Stage, Mrs Worthington," she implored. "Do not put your daughter on the Stage!"

When Madam Kemble and Betsy went to see how sweet Susan, or rather Sarah Kemble, was getting on, it was to find her deep in declamation to an impressed Third Form. "O! that this too too solid flesh would melt," the passage had started, and progressed to "But break, my heart, for I must hold my tongue!"

"Not a dry eye in the playground," gloated Betsy.

⊰ Chapter 4 ⊱

A LETTER written home from Thornloe House in 1767 by Triphemia Trip clearly sets Sarah Kemble's position in the esteem of her fellow-pupils at Mrs Hermione Worthington's Educational Establishment for the Daughters of Gentlemen.

My Dear and Honoured Mama,

I have received your letter and am truely sorry that you have had cause to complain of my remissness in keeping you informed of all our Doings —

A new pupil has been added to our number, a Miss Sarah Kemble. We had no expectation of her arrival, and at first thought her to be something of an interloper. She is very plain in her cloaths, and thought somewhat of a Brown Beauty, for her eyes and features, with the exception of a somewhat too long nose, merit much commendation. Her manner was not pleasing, withdrawing from our company and holding herself aloof from our amusements and I asked her what her parents were and what was their position, as indeed, dear Mama, you have advised me to do, to avoid the possibility of becoming intimate with an unsuitable or ungenteel acquaintance. But she answered without blush or confusion that her Father was Roger Kemble, the Actor-Manager of a troupe of Strolling Players who had arrived in the Town travelling in a waggon. You can imagine my embarrassment, my dear Mama, at having extorted so damaging a confession, and I thought it best to make a curtsy and return to the other young ladies who were awaiting my report.

To this epistle one might add a pair of poignant post post scriptums.

P.S. Miss Kemble's favourite name for Gentlemen is William —somewhat low and ordinary, we think.

P.S. Asked what her favourite name was for a Lady, Miss Kemble seemed indeterminate. Not Salubria, she said, nor Kezia. You can imagine, dear Mama, how puzzled we were. Finally, she settled on Groach which, she said, was the Given name of Lady Macbeth. Groach, if you please—whatever next!

But Sarah bore her isolation valiantly, seeming to welcome it rather than the vain chatter of her new companions. Was she thinking that the year would turn, the snow fall, and that the School Play must furnish her with her opportunity and become the touchstone of her true mettle? Or was she lost, full early before her time, in some tremulous dream of one particular William? Time will tell, and if not Time, James Boaden.

Preparations, then, were well afoot for the play that was to be crowned by a small ball thereafter, which would serve as an occasion for Prize-giving to the richer and more aristocratic girlies of Mrs Hermione Worthington's Educational Establishment. Various plays were canvassed by the Daughters of Gentlemen under the supervision of Miss Melpomene. "*The Magical Harlequinade*," Mrs Worthington's Pamela proposed. She could see herself as Columbine. "*A Midsummer Night's Dream*," offered Triphemia Tripp—"It is my honoured Mama's favourite," she sought to clinch it. She could see herself as Titania. "*The Innocent Whore?*" Sarah Kemble had produced her most thrilling tones. Miss Melpomene's hand flew to her undeniably flat chest.

"Childie, Childie," she chided, "you do not know what you are saying. At least, I hope not," she added doubtfully under her breath. Sarah Kemble failed to blush.

Finally a choice was made. *Henry the Fifth* suited everyone. Thereafter many tears were shed at rehearsals, and Mrs Worthington's Pamela—so sensitive, dear child—swooned dead away when Mrs Kemble spoke the first awe-charged line.

Some instruction in the Art of the Fan was a concomitant to the Ball which would follow the play. Sarah Kemble and the Daughters of Gentlemen were assembled in the Hall (a vast room with a ceiling painted by Angelica Kauffmann—"such a delicate talent") under the tuition of the Headmistress in person, with illustrations by Miss Melpomene.

The Headmistress rustled the parchment and placed it within eye-shot on her lectern, as an *aide memoire*. It was Addison's essay on the Language of the Fan, cut from *The Spectator* in 1711, fifty years old, and so quite suitable for the Daughters of Gentlemen.

"Women—young ladies, that is—are armed with Fans as Gentlemen with swords and sometimes do more Execution with them." Swish, Miss Melpomene had flicked open her fan.

Plomp, Miss Melpomene had dropped it. "Pick it up, dear, and continue as though nothing untoward has happened."

"She drops it every year," whispered Pamela Worthington disloyally. Miss Worthington flourished her own fan furiously.

Mrs Worthington took up her theme again:

"'To the End therefore that Ladies may be entire Mistresses'" —one of the Daughters of Gentlemen swooned. It was Adelaida Pusey—such a sensitive girlie, and so rich! Miss Melpomene closed her fan with a snap and dealt with the recumbent Miss Pusey. Mrs Worthington went on, "The girlies who carry fans under me and dear Melpomene—when she has done with— sniff—inserting feathers under Miss Pusey's nostrils—will be instructed in the use of their Arms, as was set out by Mr Addison when I was a gal—" Was she ever? The Daughters of Gentlemen found it impossible to imagine it; they fidgeted with their fans.

" 'Handle your Fans.' "

The Daughters of Gentlemen did their best.

" 'Unfurl your Fans.' "

The Daughters of Gentlemen unfurled.

" 'Discharge your Fans.' "

The Daughters of Gentlemen looked doubtfully at one another.

" 'Ground your Fans.' "

The Daughters of Gentlemen dropped their fans like hot Bath Buns.

" 'Recover your Fans.' "

Nothing for it—the Daughters of Gentlemen stooped to conquer.

" 'Flutter your Fans.' "

The Daughters of Gentlemen and the by now returned Miss Melpomene came into their own and fluttered away like giant moths around a lighted candle, bearing an entwined riband marked Matrimony.

"Flutter, girls, flutter."

The air became full of the sound of doves' wings as the Daughters of Gentlemen fluttered their fans and eyelashes.

"When my Regiment of dear Girlies is drawn up in array, with every one her Weapon in her hand, upon my word of command to Handle Fans, each shakes her Fan at me with a smile."

Ingratiatingly, Miss Melpomene shook hers and the dear girlies followed—all save one and she was no Daughter of a Gentleman.

"Daft," decided Sarah Kemble, the Strolling Thespian's daughter, borrowing the word from Betsy's vocabulary to describe her own feeling about fans used not broadly upon the boards as in *A School for Scandal*, but socially as in some soft drawing-room to which she had never penetrated, nor desired to—as yet.

"Give your right hand girlie a tap on the shoulder." The class tapped. "A tap, Miss Kemble, is not a smart rap. Class, press your lips to your extremities—the extremities of your Fans, I mean. Melpomene, my love, demonstrate—I thank you. Now, girlies, let your arms fall gently down—gently, I said, Miss Kemble. Class, stand in readiness to receive my next word of command with a closed Fan." Miss Kemble looked at the ceiling just as her Mama had done when Don Quixote had fallen off his windmill.

"Our next motion is that of unfurling our Fan in which are included several little Flirts and Vibrations, also Gradual Openings with many voluntary Fallings. This part of our exercise pleases our opposite numbers more than any other. Upon my giving the Word to Discharge your Fans, they give one crack that can be heard at some Considerable Distance when the Wind sits fair. I see several of my dear Girlies present who could not give a pop loud enough to be heard at the further end of a room." The Headmistress shook a regretful head. So did Miss Melpomene.

[34]

"I have taken thought in order to dissuade my dear Girlies from Letting Off their Fans," the Headmistress frowned, "in Highly Unsuitable Places. I have also," she patted her curls, "invented a Fan with which a Girlie of sixteen can make as loud a Crack as a Woman of fifty—even sixty. Why not?" she looked at Miss Melpomene for verification.

"Why not, indeed?" said Miss Melpomene, an obliging creature. The Headmistress looked well pleased. Miss Melpomene smirked.

"The Word of Command to 'Ground the Fan' teaches a young Lady to quit her Fan gracefully when she throws it aside." Miss Melpomene demonstrated with some energy. There was reproach in the look Mrs Worthington gave her. Exciting though the theme and its developments were, it did not do to be too enthusiastic before the Virgin Gaze—at least she hoped it was Virgin; she glanced uneasily for a moment at the poor little Kemble girlie and recollected that with that Nurse on the *qui vive* maidenhood was a certainty. Mrs Worthington, thus reassured, returned to her theme. "When the young Lady or Matron throws aside her Fan in order to take up a Pack of Cards, adjust a Curl of Hair, replace a falling Pin or apply herself to any other matter of Immediate Importance she will toss her Fan with an Air upon a long table which stands by for that purpose at fashionable functions."

The Headmistress continued the improvisation she was conducting with the unconscious Mr Addison and his interesting and informative journal, *The Spectator*. "Remind me to send the subscription," she said over her shoulder to Miss Melpomene—a mode of delivery she would never encourage the Daughters of Gentlemen to adopt. "There is an infinite Variety of Motions of which we can avail ourselves in the Flutter of the Fan: viz," said the Headmistress, the word popping out of her mouth like a pea from a shooter. "There is the Angry Flutter, the Modest Flutter—eyes down, Miss Kemble, Childie!—the Timorous

Flutter— not so bold, Miss Pusey, dear (ah, money, money—
and the Things it did to the manner of its fortunate possessors!),
the Confused Flutter, the Merry Flutter." A peal of laughter
from the once more carried-away Miss Melpomene. Mrs Worthington shook a subduing head at the wretched Miss Melpomene
who put a girlish hand before her mouth and wiped away a tear.
"And the Flutter Amorous—but that, dear Girlies, is a category
for Fifth Form and Prefects only."

"Damnation," whispered Miss Pusey.

"The Devil take the fan," hissed her bosom friend Triphemia
Tripp.

"I," continued Mrs Worthington, "have seen a Fan so very
Angry that it would have been dangerous for the Absent Lover
who provoked it to have come within wind of it, and at other times
so Amorous that I was glad for the Reputation of the Lady that
the Lover was at a sufficient distance from it."

Mrs Worthington stepped down from her lectern to a polite
patter of applause from her dear Girlies' furled Fans. Most
gratifying.

⊰ Chapter 5 ⊱

T HE Ball at Thornloe House was at its height with the
Daughters of Gentlemen a-flutter in party dresses of pale
pink, pale blue, pale lavender, pale silver grey, and also
over-insistent white. They were fanning themselves all over the
place. A great many parents had come to praise their own
genteel offspring and disparage the dear girlies of other parents.
It did not take long for Lady Loverule (for it was in her costume
that Madam Kemble was attired) to get the hang of it.

"What a pity," she said to Mrs Worthington, "the dear girlie
by the potted palm should have quite so many pimples." She
pointed. "That," said Mrs Worthington awfully, "is my daughter
Pamela." Nothing for it but a Queenly exit. Madam Kemble
executed this as swiftly as Majesty would permit.

The School Play had taken place. At the time it seemed that
the future Sarah Siddons had been right about her eventual
recognition at Thornloe House. Her duet—on two out-of-tune
harps (tiresome things, harps—they took so long a-tuning!)

with Miss Melpomene, who was gracing the night in saffron satin, though admittedly no riot or Bacchanalia, was well thought of in at least one quarter: "Well played, Melpomene," the Headmistress called out, slapping a forgetful thigh.

Even before Sarah's Thornloe House days, Roger Kemble had been determined that neither his daughter nor his elder son, jolly little Johnnie Philip, should tread the boards. But Madam Kemble decreed that singing lessons could do no harm (she was playing that energetic song-bird Mrs Peachum that night) and might come in handy. Had not her sainted Mama sung her lullabys in a rich if gin-sodden contralto? Certainly, Sarah's neat little soprano singing of some simple airs from *The Beggar's Opera* saw the School Hall warming to her—or so she felt. Only she did wish dear Mama would stop beating time with her fan in her usual large and Queenly manner, almost certainly not included in Mrs Worthington's instructive lecture on its uses.

At first glance *Henry the Fifth*, though written by the Swan of Old Avon, would seem to lie outside the scope of the young ladies of Thornloe Hall. Indeed, it had been suggested by Mrs Worthington more with an eye to her daughter's histrionic talents and Miss Melpomene's French. Miss Melpomene's French was something of a legend to successive generations of dear girlies. Fortunately the legend did not enlarge upon the quaintness of Miss Melpomene's French accent.

But Miss Adelaida Pusey had other ideas and was nothing loath to voice them. "I abominate *Henry Five*," she had said. "Why not *Macbeth*?" It was clear that she could see herself wielding the dagger. And she was so rich! Mrs Worthington suppressed a sigh. Fortunately Act One, Scene Two, line one came to her rescue. She grasped the nettle.

"I think not, dear Childie," she said. "Think of Act One, Scene Two, line one."

The dear girlies gazed at their Headmistress with puzzled eyes. Not so the future Sarah Siddons who was well acquainted with the text. "What bloody man is this?" she quoted in ringing tones.

Let us leave her to write five hundred lines of *Paradise Lost*. Finally the choice fell on *Henry the Eighth*, in which Miss Pusey would play the eponymous anti-hero, and Miss Kemble, still rather inky, would give her Cardinal Wolsey.

Never can the Cardinal have been injected with quite so many alternative roles. Generous to a fault, Sarah threw into that staid, politicking, scarlet gentleman so many of her dear Parent's characterisations. At one point she invested him with her Lady Macbeth; at another it was The Grecian Daughter, then Juliet, Henry the Fourth and Richard Crookback. By the time she had arrived in thrilling tones at "Farewell, a long farewell to all my Greatness," the Daughters of Gentlemen were swooning like knocked-over nine-pins. Several Mamas in the audience had taken to their smelling-salts and even Papas were swallowing hard, and sniffing snuff. Yes, Miss Kemble had indeed made her effect.

In the back row — late again — a thin, bespectacled, very young second cousin of one of the dear girlies was looking elated. He recognised passages from the Lady, of course, and Richard Crookback. But who was this Grecian Daughter? Certainly, her attitude was magnificent even though tonight she was wrapped around and practically extinguished by Cardinal Wolsey's scarlet flannel cloak (or would do for Dick Whittington's Pa-in-law).

For all the speeches from other plays inserted whenever a principal forgot a line, which was the high custom in barn-storming circles (indeed it is on record that two actresses with other matters on their minds ran through speeches from four other plays in strict common form with considerable resource,

[39]

until they got themselves back to their original play), James Boaden was in a mood to congratulate himself upon the lucky cousin who had undertaken to sponsor him at Mrs Worthington's Academy. Not a dry eye in the Assembly Hall, he noted happily.

He even stayed on through the Prize-Giving. Miss Kemble stepped up to receive her copy of Milton's poems to a crescendo of applause. Even in her salad days—when she was but ten years old, to be precise—she had read her *Paradise Lost* and was to treasure it for the rest of her life. There would come the time when she would refuse to play Cleopatra, for soon she would be afraid of what such passion would do to her day-to-day character, preferring the more feline Lady Macbeth, which one day she would make her own. Like Anna Lovely in *A Bold Stroke for a Wife*, she greatly feared the flesh and the weakness thereof!

In the ante-room used on more mundane occasions for Scripture (Miss Melpomene) Miss Adelaida Pusey's dear Mama (so rich) was glaring at a long Queen Anne red lacquer table, placed there to lodge the ladies' fans. Mrs Pusey was a hasty lady, given to making instant wrong decisions. She herself would never have given that old-fashioned table house-room, she decided, and Mr Hepplewhite could mind his own business! She kicked it . . .

❧ Chapter 6 ❧

THE two years, spent at times in disgrace, and at times in adulation, sped by. When her schooldays' star was rising Sarah would be taken to town by the visiting parents of some more fortunate—for so it must have seemed to others at that time—Daughters of Gentlemen, there to gorge on Sunday delicacies washed down, as Betsy Noakes would say, by cans of hot chocolate, served in Mr Wedgwood's classical-pattern china. Or one of the Day Girlies might bring her in some freshly baked Butter Cakes, a local delicacy that she remembered years later: "I could eat a dozen at a time," she was to say, wistfully. To outward seeming, Sarah, at that time, had become a young lady of fourteen, on the way to fifteen, fit to grace Mrs Worthington's Establishment and the Royal College of Preceptors.

Soon it would be spring and the seasons would have brought round the Worcester Races. It was therefore time for the Kembles to set up their stage in the field that bordered the course. On Saturday night Madam Kemble gave her Cleopatra to her husband's highly proper and very suitable Anthony. Nannie Noakes would have given her Iras in white calico and streamers of simulated seaweed (which did, too, for Mad Tilburina's even madder Confidante—less suitable and something of a pity). On Sunday the two good ladies called to collect Sarah—as pretty a maid as you could see this side of the Cattle Market. It was time for her to resume her career under the loving but strict scrutiny of her parents and the even stricter scrutiny of Nannie Noakes. Time for her, too, to resume her distant but fascinated gazing at William Siddons, the better to do which she would arm herself with a metal candlestick and a pair of snuffers and clatter them together in the Sides to make the whirling sails of the windmill in the Harlequinade more realistic whenever William Siddons was playing Harlequin. How she envied Salubria Golightly, a lanky sixteen-year-old, who in her own absence at Thornloe House had been promoted to play Columbine.

A word about William Siddons. James Boaden was to write of him that "he could play anything from Hamlet to Harlequin", and who are we to doubt his considered verdict? The first public announcement that he had joined the Kembles was to be found on a playbill in the Worcester Chymist's bay-window—where else?—dated February 1st, 1767. The bill, among other fascinating attractions, held out a performance of *King Charles the First* at the Worcester Theatre—a stable in the back yard of the King's Head, the Hostelry opposite the Town Hall:

DUKE OF RICHMOND, Mr Siddons.

It wasn't much, but it was a start, and more to Mr Siddons' taste than being a barber's apprentice—his first tussle with life—or a tapster at his father's snug little pub, The London Apprentice, in Rushall Street, Walsall. His sole appearance, one gathers, before donning the Ducal Coronet, was as an amateur helping out in a play in the Malt House of Mr Samuel Wood on the Lime-Pit bank. James Boaden further assures us that, at this stage of his career, Sid was "a fair and very handsome man, sedate and graceful in his manners". Certainly his good looks had their effect on the fourteen-year-old Sarah, too young grown-up in what Thornloe House had taught her was a rough, harsh world. Not quite fitting into either Mrs Worthington's *ambiance* nor the crudeness of the Strollers' paint and rushlight, it had not been the easiest of transitions for Sarah from the young-ladyhood of Mrs Worthington's Academy to the coarser, more exciting world of a would-be Juliet. Before the two years of civilising at Thornloe House she had been a talented but tousled child whom William Siddons could pat on the head before continuing on his unthinking way. But now the player-urchin had returned to the Strollers a young, a very young, lady with that mixture of common-sense and sensitivity—a mixture that was to stand her in good stead in years to come when she led a strolling company of her own—and indeed for the rest of her career. Siddons awarded her an elaborate flourish of his hat, part mocking, part in admiration. Once when she had given her first Titania, he had kissed her hand in an emotional moment of congratulation; that hand which but for Nannie Noakes' scandalised insistence would have gone unwashed for many a night, so dearly did she cherish that lightly-given kiss.

"Now then, Sairey, none of your Capulet nonsense. Cleanliness is next to Godliness—that's what my Mama taught me. She may not have been sainted like some other Mama's Mamas I could mention, but she was as good and God-fearing a woman as you could find in a day's strolling, before the gin got at her."

And there was no gainsaying Nannie Noakes now or ever. Sarah trailed the very tips of her fingers in the basin and comforted herself with the thought that many waters could not quench love.

The Sides, wherever the stage chanced to be set up, were always crowded when the Kembles were giving *The Dream*. The usual clutter of cast were doing their wing-work, elbowing two junior sprites out of their way. Kezia Quicktobed and Salubria Golightly were used to being bundled off.

"Titania indeed!" Kezia sounded resentful. As usual. She herself was playing a rather plump Mounseer Mustard Seed on this occasion.

"She'll be getting a Benefit all to herself before you can say Two Gentlemen of Verona," Salubria, a lank and, to tell the truth, rather squeaky Puck foretold.

"All airs and graces," jeered the plump Mustard Seed.

"She'll get her come-uppance, you mark my words," the lanky Puck proclaimed. "That's if she hasn't had it already," she finished darkly.

"Had it already?"

"Someone we know held my hand last night all through the Love Juice scene. I expect we shall be announcing our engagement soon."

For a moment Mustard Seed thought of switching her jealousy. But only for a moment, for Puck continued thrillingly: "You should have seen Someone Else we know's pallor when I told her!"

"White as a sheet?"

"White like she'd swounded dead away."

"Like she swound to the ground?" Mustard Seed was hungry for details.

"No. But she staggered, like this—and . . ."

"Steady on, young lady," said a much put-out Bottom. He glared: "You'll have me off the bloody boards."

". . . and she had to pretend she'd caught her foot in her petticoats!"

"Serves her right!"

"Show-off," they agreed.

In the opposite Sides their respective Mamas were discussing Madam Kemble's Hypolita, on-stage and Giving, even as they spoke, or rather hissed.

"Buskins indeed!" Zenobia Quicktobed addressed herself to the barn ceiling, or rather the hole in the barn ceiling, "and those underskirts draped to give a glimpse of her thighs." Peg Golightly drew up her underskirt to show her own.

"That'll fascinate 'em," said Zenobia. She winked.

"And at her age!"

"Show-off," they agreed.

They paused in their gossip to memorise, feverishly, Helena and Hermia's lines in a wood near Athens; lines with which they had but the customary Strollers' nodding acquaintance to instant memory. Ever since the awful, never-to-be-forgotten occasion in a stable-yard in Hereford when they had lost their way in Another Part of the Island, and had been forced to find their way back to Shakespeare via lavish helpings from other writers' plays, speech for speech, *The Dream*, too, had become a dreaded nightmare to Zenobia and Peg, but not until Peg had volunteered the comment to the hole in the roof: "Sainted Mama be damned!"

On-stage Hypolita was preparing to make her customary sweeping exit, arms flung to the high heavens.

"Four Days will swiftly steep themselves in Night," she declaimed as one might make a funeral oration, when suddenly an over-ripe tomato, hurled in condemnation of her reading, mysteriously changed course in mid-air and hit Zenobia making her entrance, with a nasty wet squelch.

"That'll learn her," said an inebriated voice through that convenient hole in the roof of the barn. "Hic!" it added, or so the muttering Zenobia, hastily dabbing her cheek, could have sworn.

⊶ Chapter 7 ⊷

CLEOPATRA was making-up before a looking-glass illumined by no less than four candle-stubs, in a real theatre in the Maddermarket. Cleopatra was frowning. This was not because she could not seem to soot the shadows of her countenance in the right places, but, Cleopatra reminded herself, before everything she was a Mother, just as her Sainted Mama had been before her. Somehow today her eyebrows refused to meet, no matter how much black shoe-polish she applied. Beside her Betsy Noakes was chunnering on.

It transpired that from out of a day-dream Sarah had twice called her "William". Nannie Noakes summed it up: "The poor lamb's growing up and is now of an age to be influenced by flourishes and hand-kissings."

"Hand-kissings," said Cleopatra awfully. "Pa will have to settle this. He must give Mr Siddons his congé from the Company. I'll have him tumbled out of our circuit like a cheese."

"Before his Benefit?"

"We will advance his Benefit Night and be rid of him by Michaelmas—'for Brutus', Mr Kemble that is, 'is an honourable man', and it has been promised. And furthermore I will have a word with my Attendant, Charmian."

"You mean your daughter, Sairey," said Nannie Noakes, who had no patience with artistic inexactitudes. "I will send young Sairey to you as soon as she dies."

It did not take Sarah long to die and scamper off at the end of the play. If Mama had sent for her amidst the scurry of packing-up when all hands were needed it had to be something important. Sarah removed her make-up with lamb's fat and ran in, only to find her Mama in one of her perilous calms—the Kemble family's usual way of unwinding after a taxing part.

"Oh Mama, is it—it must be—my Portia at last?"

In the Trial Scene Sarah played Nerissa, with a dear little moustache and a wig with side-curls which pleased her mightily, but she longed to give her reading of Portia's "Quality of Mercy" speech.

"No," said Cleopatra with a firmness that went quite some way to belie the deepness of her trance. She herself played Portia.

"Back to Nerissa," sighed Sarah, "again next Tuesday at Brecon, the town of my birth!" As though Cleopatra ever could forget the primitive conditions attendant upon a first birth at the Shoulder of Mutton Inn at Brecon.

"You know, Daughter, that neither I nor Papa wish you to undergo the hardships that your parents and their parents have had to suffer."

"But," said her daughter, "we come of a strolling family: a pomping family!"

"Born to it," the muffled voice of Betsy Noakes floated out of the depths of the wicker basket into which she was bent double, pressing down sundry robes suitable for Roman Matrons and Christian Martyrs, to make room for Cleopatra's vast breast-plate and head-dresses and the respectably draped lengths in which Cleopatra wound her considerable self. There should have been ample room for all, since it was into this very laundry basket that the most gentlemanly Sir John Falstaff in the length and breadth of the land was wont to bestow himself, dirty washing and all.

"That," said Cleopatra, discarding a clonking great bracelet (or would do for the Queens of England), "is as it may be. But loving and"—she emphasised—"watchful parents know what is best for their daughters."

"But," said Sarah, "I am an Attraction."

"Attraction is it, Miss?" Cleopatra's patrician nose cleaved the air. She sniffed.

But her daughter stood her ground. "The public weep when I weep. And when I die the ladies swound—swoon," she corrected herself.

The daughter of Old Nile dispensed with an ear-ring—she had been dying to take off the plaguey thing all evening. "Mama and Papa know what is best for you and your brother John Philip, the merry little prankster," she said. Betsy, sorting out some well-trampled shoes, sniffed audibly.

"But I'm improving all the time—even Master Boaden says so."

"That clumsy beanpole," said Nannie Noakes, "always turning up like a bad half-groat, as the saying is."

"Mama knows best," said Cleopatra, "just as Mama's Mama knew best."

"But you eloped with Papa, didn't you? And you've lived happily ever after."

Cleopatra and Betsy looked at one another and if a look could speak Betsy's would have been saying, "That is what comes of too much book-learning."

"Daughters!" Cleopatra sighed. And if a sigh had an echo, somewhere in the regions of the ceiling that sigh would have been duplicated in ghostly agreement.

[48]

Later that night at the Inn Madam Kemble called a council of war over a mulling of negus, well spiced and piping hot, the council being composed of her good husband, her good self, and a resentful Betsy Noakes.

"It is high time that we took steps to safeguard the brightest jewel in our crown — our daughter Sarah," she announced.

"It is high time we all went to bed if you ask me!" muttered Nannie Noakes who needed her eight hours of sleep, come haystack, come hedgerow — the said sleep being the only peace she was likely to enjoy from morn till all hours of the night.

Madam Kemble ignored the broad hint. "It has long been agreed," she said, "that neither Sarah nor Johnnie-Philip are to follow our family on to the Boards."

"Allow me to remind you, Dear Spouse, that it is indeed to this end that we will be sending John Philip to a Benedictine establishment at Douai at Michaelmas."

Nanny Noakes muttered something definitive and sexual which did little for the Benedictine image in France or any other country. Nannie Noakes did not hold with Popish Practices whatsoever they might be. Fortunately Sairey had been brought up a Christian, like her Mama. There was comfort in the thought for Betsy Noakes. "And Johnnie such a merry little fellow," she mourned.

"I," said Madam Kemble, "have been caringly advised, through the kind offices of a friend of a friend of our family, to send Daughter Sarah into the service of the Widow Greatheed of Guy's Cliffe — an establishment of the first distinction only just short of Royalty itself," almost Madam Kemble's voice genuflected, "where she can be of use to the daughterless Widow, Lady Greatheed, and keep her hands off Portia or any of the heavy roles in the imperishable plays of Mrs Aphra Benn for that matter, and where, in return for the bestowal of her companionship in the drawing-room, and a little plain sewing and needle-neat darning in the still-room, and a deal of reading aloud to her Ladyship, no doubt from the classics, she shall be treated quite as one of the family and shall learn many Lady-like refinements."

"Our Sairey has been sent away from us already, and what did lady-like refinements do for her? Narry a thing," Nannie Noakes answered herself, "save send her back to us all the more wilful and love-lorn."

"Love?" Roger Kemble sounded startled. "Can our girlie be in love already? Surely not. She is but a child."

"She is well-nigh seventeen, husband. Younger than that are maidens Mothers made. And in many ways it might be better to send her away, out of the range of fire."

"Out of sight, out of mind," mused Roger Kemble.

"Not that I hold with her whims and fancies," said Betsy, "but a daughter's place is in the home. Her parents' home."

"We have no home," said Madam Kemble. "We are Thespians. Besides, the friend of my friend informs me that at Guy's Cliffe there is a son of the house, at least a brother, and who knows ..." she finished darkly.

"Who indeed?" agreed her husband.

"The Lord knows," muttered Betsy.

The candle guttered. Betsy's eyes blinked, then closed. Her head nodded. "She is asleep, poor soul," said Madam Kemble, helping the finest Coriolanus on the circuit and her good self handsomely from the negus cup. And there they sat on in the light of the fire considering their children's future, like any Mother and Father in the family farmhouse the length and breadth of the kingdom, fortifying themselves against what the future might hold.

Suddenly the peace of the night was shattered by a great thundering at the door of the Inn.

"Mercy on us," exclaimed the woken-up and thoroughly disgruntled Betsy, "whoever can it be?"

"And at this hour!" exclaimed Madam Kemble. The two

women regarded each other with the unanimity of a Greek Chorus.

They were soon to know for there was a shuffling of boots and a clumping of heavy bolts at the front door, the sound of voices raised in argument, the unceremonious flinging open of their very door and young Mr Siddons, flushed and dishevelled for he too had been fortifying himself, stood in the aperture and addressed himself to Roger Kemble.

"I have come to secure your permission to press my suit with your daughter Sarah," he said.

᪷ Chapter 8 ᪷

SEVERAL Titanias to William Siddon's Oberon and not a
few handmaidens to her Mama's Cleopatra had flowed
under Sarah's bridge since Siddons — Sid to the company —
had mindlessly held Salubria Golightly's grubby little paw in the
love-juice scene; mainly because the grubby little paw had been
so tenacious. Days filled with the sweet young burgeoning of
Sarah's beauty, her courageous, even thrilling acting, and their
irresistible closeness in their scenes together. Siddons, who had
been more or less flung into leading roles before he was a mature
actor, was prudently conscious that it would be no mean thing to
inherit a father-in-law's Circuit and troupe of Thespians, and
had done nothing to discourage Sarah's rising star.

Madam Kemble, aided and abetted by Betsy Noakes, had
kept a Mother's strict eye on the little romance which stood in
the way of her vision of Sarah as future mistress of Guy's Cliffe
(white satin — Princess of France, *Henry the Fifth*) and of
herself as Bride's Mother (something purple — Volumnia,

Coriolanus). On more than one occasion she had instructed Sarah to raise her sights.

And it had happened on the evening of his unceremonious breaking in upon the Kembles' peace that Madam Kemble had sent for her daughter, when the play was done, to admonish her before that worthy lady's perilous calm had set in.

"I have noticed, Daughter, that in spite of my frequently delivered and specific instructions that you should take note of the disposal of the gentry in the house . . ."

"Barn!" Sarah, knowing perfectly well what was to follow from many similar exhortations, was already at her most defiant.

"Have you not noted, Daughter, that we set up at increasingly fewer rural barns and make-do stages of late? More often than not we have been playing in a suitably intimate Theatre Royal or a sufficiently large Town Hall, I'll have you know, Miss. Or is it that you have been too carried away by your roles in our Tragedies to care?" Madam Kemble, wearied though she was by Lady Restless (*All in the Wrong*), lowered the left eyebrow and drew down one corner of her lips, expressive of irony, and shamelessly borrowed from her Ariadne face (*The Rival Sisters*). "Have you not observed that when I perceive a titled lady or the wife of a squire of some substance, and when they have been gracious enough to applaud at the end of a soliloquy, I pay tribute to their courtesy by halting the traffic of the stage while I curtsy to them."

"I have," said Sarah. Could that dryness of articulation denote disapproval? At her age? And aimed at the most passionate Cleopatra on the Circuit? Madam Kemble drew a deep breath.

"It is my intention that you should follow my example."

"But Mama—in the middle of a scene!"

"Precisely. Politeness to the influential is no Bubble. Its argosies return, sooner or later, with benefit to all concerned."

"But Mama . . ."

"But me no buts, Miss."

"But—I mean, in a comedy when I am playing some country serving wench, or the maid to some great lady, I can bob a saucy little curtsy with no great loss of—" she sought for the word—"atmosphere, but in a tragedy when I am fired, and the audience weeps with me . . ."

"Comedy, Tragedy, Pastoral Comedy . . ." it was Madam Kemble's turn now to pause for a word. She found it. "Fiddlesticks!"

"But soon I am to play Euphrasia. Papa has promised me *The Grecian Daughter*."

"Nothing of the sort. Soon you are to be sent into service to be kept out of harm's way."

"But Mama, I get so carried away, and so does my Public."

"You'll not get carried away at Guy's Cliffe. Nor will your brother John Philip when the monks get him."

Sarah's eyes filled with tears for her own and her jolly little brother's bleak future.

"And so, for the brief time you tread our boards, take heed of my instructions, Miss."

"B-but my Motivation . . . !"

Sarah's tears brooked no denial. Weeping she ran from the room, and as it so happened, straight into Sid's astonished arms.

Comforting led to embracing; embracing to kissing; kissing to a shared ecstasy. For over the ecstatic weeks an intimacy had grown, which accounted for the tousled figure of William Siddons in the doorway of the Kembles' lodgings at the inn, where the candle guttered but the flames of the fire in the hearth leapt, and the Kembles were dumbfounded. By the time they came to, Sid was repeating, "To press my suit with your daughter. In short, to marry Sarah."

"Over Roger Kemble's dead body," Madam Kemble declared, "is that not so, Husband?"

"Well . . ." said Roger Kemble, weakly.

⊷ Chapter 9 ⊷

POOR Mr Siddons. The parental interview proved sharp and
disillusioning. Into it Madam Kemble put any of her tart
performances as Kate the Shrew to shame! As for the
most gentlemanly Petruchio from Land's End to John O'Groats,
his own courting days came back to him with unaccustomed
vividness. When Roger Kemble had asked his prospective
Pa-in-law for his daughter's hand in honourable marriage, had
not the worthy Mr Ward roared that he would be damned
before he would allow a daughter of his to marry some actor—
and he himself the Actor Manager at the head of a travelling
troupe on a well established Circuit! Even worse was to follow.
Mr Ward went on roaring that in the unlikely event of his
taking leave of his own senses and sanctioning such a match,
his daughter would be marrying a man who was no actor.
Roger and Madam Kemble eloped.

Now roaring was quite outside Roger Kemble's effects unless,
of course, he was playing the most gentlemanly Bottom in *The*

Dream. But recollecting the effect on him his Pa-in-law's poor opinion of his acting had caused, he tried to ease the situation by throwing a fresh log on the fire, while recollecting his late Pa-in-law's attitude aloud. Madam Kemble looked at him. There was a strong reminder of Lady Macbeth in that look, a little touch of Constance in the night, and more than a little of Hermione (*The Distressed Mother*).

In short, young William Siddons was given his congé, to be implemented the morning after his promised Benefit.

Do not imagine that Sarah, their usually docile daughter, found no argument against her wonderful Sid's rejection and banishment, nor that she did not borrow much of her material from the Montagues and the Capulets. She fumed. She pleaded. She wept. She braved her parents both together and separately. She refused her food and lost a deal of weight. She looked pale, and even under the stage rouge she made a wan Sweet Ann Page with scarce the spirit for a romp with the Merry Wives of Windsor. She shrieked—Mad Margaret could not have sounded shriller. She sulked. She stormed. She swooned away all over Breconshire, in which county the pomping folk were parading. And she fair drove Nannie Noakes to Bedlam. As for young Sid, he kept his outraged feelings to himself and simmered a dark revenge, which was to see the light of late afternoon at Brecon, the bustling little county town, where the ladies, bless 'em, took a keen and particular interest in Sarah's progress and felt her to be one of themselves, though heaven-endowed.

At this time, in his all too short salad days, William Siddons was a rash young man, though at a later date he was to act as good sound ballast to his young wife's temperament.

The pomping parade at Brecon took place to applause from lined streets. The sharp eyes of the Brecon ladies noted the good looks and dashing address of Madam Kemble's *jeune premier*. There was a concerted rush of ladies to the primitive but licensed theatre, to acquire seats for themselves and their good men.

There was no question but that there would be a full house for William Siddons' Benefit.

Just as it had taken parental opposition to confirm Sarah in her passionate belief that all the heroic virtues abided in the breast of this nonpareil of every hero there had ever been—her Sid—so the ladies of Brecon, at his instigation, formed solid ranks on his side. For the hurt pride of the mediocre arose within him, and on the night of his Benefit he laid bare all his woes to the good wives of Brecon—in iambic pentameters, under the fashionable guise of "poor Colin, a lover *discarded*" and, less than fairly, disclosed his driving fear that:

> "She [Sarah] acquainted her Ma, who, her ends to obtain,
> Determined poor Colin to drive from the plain."

in which he continued in this stance for some nine verses, which included the hurtful lines:

> "A jilt is the Devil, as has long been confessed
> Which a heart like poor Colin must ever detest."

Upon which our Sarah, docile in all save her proposed marriage, obediently sang the ballad she was set down to perform:

> "No, no, no,
> Sweet Robin you shall not go;
> Where, you wanton, could you be
> Half so happy as with me?"

and swooned dead away, as indeed did many of the ladies in her audience.

Up in the gallery a tall, lean youth wiped away his tears. What a stroke of luck 'twas that the College of Preceptors was holding its annual examinations in Brecon, and that he was sitting at them on the very afternoon of William Siddons' Benefit. It will come as no shock to the Reader of Sensibility that this spindly youth with the ink-stained handkerchief was that very same James Boaden who, a handful of years later, was to write of Sarah Siddons that "Her Rosalind seemed indeed to be brought up by a great magician and to be forest-born. It was one of her most delicate achievements," he was to maintain in the face of dissident criticism. "The graceful Farewell to Orlando was in such a style of comedy as could only come from a spirit tenderly touched." And he was to continue: "It might at first be thought that her figure would not express the fragility (it might indeed be thought!) of this lovely sacrifice to her affections — but the height was diminished by lowering the head-dress and the *countenance* permitted not the eye to be discursive."

⊷ Chapter 10 ⊱

AND so, palpitating and vibrant with some inner fire, Sarah was sent to Lady Greatheed at Guy's Cliffe, in Warwick, there to arrange the flowers and light the candles in the echoing dining-room, to read aloud to Her Ladyship from Lord Chesterfield's *Letters*, and, or so we are told, passionately spout Milton in the servants' hall from a book of his poems given to her by the Greatheeds, the lady of the house and her susceptible brother, and all for £10 a year.

At Guy's Cliffe she was permitted to correspond with her Sid, who was even allowed to visit her from time to time. It was her father who obtained this dispensation, for he could refuse his graceful Sarah nothing—save her Mother's Roles.

Here, in the harmonious atmosphere of Guy's Cliffe, Sarah's nature blossomed into a sensitivity—and her features flowered into beauty. Her future firmness was as yet the merest hint, and lay in the majesty with which she held her head. Indeed Lady Greatheed once admitted that she used always to feel an irresistible inclination to rise from her chair when her Queenly dependent came into the room.

And the gentle days passed by, punctuated only by the infrequent visits of her Sid, who entered through the back door, and his letters, and those she would write him in return. It was a world of candlelight and glittering silver, a world of flowering chintz, a polite world, filled with well-modulated voices. Here words were given time to expand, and thought was allowed its full measure of silence.

Even the mouldings on the doors, Sarah Siddons was to tell her daughters, were, to her, a liberal education. So closely did the Queenly little maid resemble a daughter of the house that Lady Greatheed said to her brother, Lord Brownlow Bertie, who had been a thought too warm about her readings from Milton and Macbeth: "Brother, do not encourage the gal or we will have her going back to the stage."

And so, happily, instructively and peacefully, two years slipped away in this haven of politesse, and it was time for Sarah to wed her Sid.

Accordingly in 1773 her parents gave their slow consent, and on November 26th of that year the young couple, as Sir Peter Teazle so well puts it, became involved in matrimony. The ceremony was conducted in the presence of Roger and Madam Kemble, the latter looking remarkably handsome arrayed in Gertrude's richest gown—too many Volumnias had worn away the sheen on the proposed purple plush, and The Bride's mother stood, like Niobe, all tears, supported by Nannie Noakes, in Lady Montague's olive-green gown bordered by rat's fur. The Bride's Procession was notable, apart from her own ivory radiance, for two bridesmaids from her Pa's company.

"I cannot imagine what he sees in her," whispered Salubria Golightly.

"Money," murmured Kezia Quicktobed darkly, in which she spoke more prophetically than she knew.

[60]

◦⊰ Chapter 11 ⊱◦

"Have you ever," wrote Garrick to John Moody, the ideal stage-Irishman of his days, "heard of a woman, Siddons, who is strolling somewhere near you?"

Garrick was constantly on the lookout for new faces and promising players for Drury Lane, and kept at hand a number of the *cognoscenti*, both actors and seasoned playgoers, to advise him.

The Bridal Couple had begun by toiling round Roger Kemble's well-trodden circuit—Worcester, Hereford, Monmouth, Brecon, Stratford—strolling as far to the north as Leeds and Sheffield, and to the south as Devizes; Sarah satisfying her unremitting passion for tragedy queens with crumbs from Madam Kemble's well-stocked table of "heavies" as well as the Queens of Comedy and pert wenches which even Madam Kemble felt to be no longer suitable to her own stature. The darker discards proved, however, to be parts in which Sarah could reduce the refined ladies of the spas to streams of tears, audible sobs and fits of swooning, while her Sid was banished to his Pa-in-law's candle-countings and Benefit accountings.

At Devizes, one evening, by the spluttering log and fluctuating candlelight in the Bear Inn, where the luck of the Kembles and Sid's careful accounting had furnished the Royal Family of Strollers with lodgings for the night, the door of the parlour swung open to admit a small boy, a beautiful child of five or six, bestriding a painted wooden hobby-horse, who rode it round the long dark table two or three times, and toppled over at the feet of the loveliest vision he had ever seen. Soon he had picked himself up and set to work with his coloured chalks at a most amazing likeness of Sarah Siddons. It was the admiration of all who gazed at it in the leaping light in the old Inn parlour, which in no way surprised the boy's proud father, the Innkeeper, a lapsed parson and former man-of-law of the name of Lawrence, whose regulars were always calling for "Master Tom", demanding that he should paint their portrait or spout long passages of Shakespeare or Milton or both.

Sometimes the past casts a long shadow into the future. Sarah Siddons thought at times of the boy on the painted hobby-horse; that beautiful boy with the blond curls and pale complexion who, in the years to come, was to be her own delight and the doom of her lovely daughters.

Before long Sarah decided to leave the affectionate nursery of her father's circuit, and to go first to Joseph Younger's troupe, hoping that here her beloved Sid would be properly appreciated as an actor, and then, when her patience was spent, to Chamberlain and Crump's Company where her Sid — perhaps it was as well, for what family would not have been rent apart by two highly charged talents, in conflict? — settled for managing her, and book-keeping for the company, in which he must have been transparently honest, and where at last Sarah was allowed to give her Portia.

It was, however, to *Venice Preserved* that Lord Bruce and

his step-daughter with the taking name of the Honourable Henrietta Boyle, dropped in to the Cheltenham Theatre "in a mood of indulgent good humour". The sophisticated step-father and daughter were in fond hopes of sharing a fit of ill-bred giggles, or at least half-hiding well-bred smiles at the antics and attitudes of the highly-coloured creatures behind the floats. Now, though stunningly youthful, Mrs Siddons' Belvidera was a swoon-jerker if ever there was one. Had she not stood in the Sides to watch her not-yet-Sainted because-still-very-much-alive Mama's Belvidera, all paint and passion, bursting the stitches to her bodice with the heavings of her bosom? And although the Bride of but a handful of months was less luxuriant in this direction, already she was pregnant with her son Henry, which must have given her a fair enough generosity thereabouts.

Miss Boyle surprised even herself by crying so hard over Sarah's pathos and tender years that the sound of her sobs convinced the young tragedienne, who was naturally enough at her most sensitive, that she was being mocked, and she hurried home "in an agony of vexation". In view of her daughter's interesting condition, Madam Kemble had persuaded her husband to dispense with the services of Betsy Noakes—of use though the years had made her in the Kemble repertoire—to accompany Sarah as she herself had been accompanied upon Sarah's birth: and Nannie Noakes, noting the state of her weeping charge, set about half-scolding, half-comforting her.

"There, there," she said, "what a lot of fuss about play-acting. And you with someone else to think for soon. All that mouthing and blather cannot be good for the poor Babe, unable as yet to see the light of day, and if you ask me, it's a good thing I'm here to see it sensible and settled."

The following morning, Lord Bruce, walking in Cheltenham, met William Siddons. He bowed, Sid bowed. Lord Bruce selected a few well-chosen words of compliment to be conveyed from him to the promising young Belvidera of the night before.

"What words of praise from a noble Lord would seem other than well-chosen?" asks Mrs Parsons, who, save for James Boaden far away in the future, was to be Sarah's most discursive biographer — discursive, but of a quiet wit withal.

Soon we find the Honourable Miss Henrietta Boyle calling on Mrs Siddons at her lodging — a kindness the First Lady of the Boards was never to forget, and indeed dwelt on in her retirement.

> That lovely, generous and sweet creature, then in her eighteenth year, encouraged and soothed me, and indeed was unremitting in every kind and delicate attention to my feelings and wishes, nay even condescended to make part of my dresses with her own hand, and forgetting her high rank, even to assume the character of Directress of my Wardrobe.

Mrs Siddons was by now reaching her time. She dropped her first born, Henry, in the wings in true Kemble tradition at the Theatre Royal in Worcester. She was twenty years old.

The weeks took wing. County town succeeded county town.

The bassinet that once coddled the future Sarah Siddons now stood in the wings bearing her little son.

We can imagine, then, that Lord Bruce would lose no time in communicating to Garrick his good opinion of his new-found Goddess of the Buskins and imagine that the great little man, or, as his envious enemies — and they were many — spoke of him, the little great man, should send for her to show her paces.

Garrick, nearing the close of his reign at Drury Lane, ever found it hard to refuse a Lord. Moreover it might well prove to be a chastening thing to throw the cat, or, in view of the lissom youth of Mrs Siddons, the kitten among the pigeons in the flaunting forms of Mrs Abingdon, nigh on forty, Mrs Yates forty-eight, and Miss Young, who suitably enough was still youthful, all of them with the very devil of a will of their own and all of whom he would cheerfully consign to Satan, when the weather at the Lane was inclement, and when was it not?

And so we find him writing to the Reverend Henry Bate, Proprietor of *The Morning Post*, Master of Fox Hounds, and prime green-room gossip:

> If you pass by Cheltenham in your way to Worcester I wish you would see an actress there, a Mrs Siddons. She has a desire to try her Fortune with Us. Pray desire to know upon what conditions she would make her tryal . . .

The Reverend Henry Bate, whom James Boaden was later — much later — to describe as "lay in his manners" duly reported:

> After combatting the various difficulties of one of the cussedest cross-roads in the Kingdom, we arrived safe at Cheltenham . . . and saw the theatrical heroine of that place in the character of Rosalind: though I beheld her from the side wings of the stage (a barn about three yards over and consequently under almost every disadvantage) . . . I think she cannot fail to be a valuable acquisition to Drury Lane . . .

Having just admired Sarah's figure which he described as "remarkably fine, when she is happily delivered of a big belly", for by now she was again *enceinte* this time of the lovely, unselfish, delicate and most gentle, tragic Sally Siddons, "which entirely mars for the present her entire shape," (it would do!) the Reverend Master of Fox Hounds and owner of *The Morning Post* continues:

> Her face . . . is one of the most strikingly beautiful for stage effect that ever I beheld . . . in short I know of no

C   [65] woman who marks the different passages and transitions with so much variety and propriety of expression.

He then, truthful parson if green-room gossip, admitted that her voice was "rather dissonant", but hastened to add that she had contracted "no strolling habits" (shades of her not yet Sainted Mama).

She has a good "breeches figure" . . . Nay, beware yourself, great little man, for she plays Hamlet to the satisfaction of the Worcestershire Critics . . .

With wisdom beyond her years and somewhat to the annoyance of her Sid, Sarah refused to state her terms but left them to Garrick's generosity. Bate continued to press eloquently on her behalf.

I remain, my Dr Sir, (after writing a Damned jargon of unintelligable stuff in haste)

Ever yours most truly etc

P.S. Direct to me at the Hop Pole.

Directed to him at the Hop Pole, as requested, back came Garrick's reply:

Dear Bate:

Ten thousand thanks for your very clear, agreeable and friendly letter; it pleased me much; and whoever calls it *a jargon* of *unintelligable stuff* should be knocked down if I were near him [An imagined cartoon of the great little man on a beanstalk squaring up to an actor's head springs irresistibly to mind.] I most desire you to secure the lady with very best compliments and say that she may depend upon every

reasonable and friendly encouragement in my power ...
You must intimate to the husband that he must be satisfy'd
with *the state of life in which it has pleased Heaven to call her.*

Your account of the Big belly alarms me! When will she
be in shape again? How long does the lady count? ... I
should be glad to know her cast of parts ... above all, my
dear Farmer, let me know at what time she may reckon to
lye-in.

Back comes the Reverend M.F.H's answer:

... I found it unnecessary to make the intimation you
desired to the *husband* since he requires only to be employ'd
in any role you shall think proper ... I saw him the other
evening in Young Marlow in Goldsmith's comedy, and then
he was far from despicable; neither his figure nor face contemptible ... Now for the *Big Belly* [continued the Country
Cleric, not one assumes, without a certain lay relish], She has
already gone *six months* so that pretty early in December she
will be fit for service ... I am strongly for her 1st appearance
in *Rosalind.*

and he proceeded to append a list of roles, underscoring Sarah's
preferences.

Jane Shore	Minimia	Lady Townley
Alicia	Juliet	Portia
Roxana Daughter	Horatio R Falk	Violante
Matilda	Marianne	Rosalind
Belvidera	Imogen	Mrs Strickland
Calista	Charlotte	Clarissa
	Widow Brady	Miss Aubrey

As they are ready to attend your summons at any time, they

ask whether they are not to be allowed something to subsist upon when they come to town, previous to her appearance?

Whether you have any objection to employ *him* in any situation, in which you think him likely to be useful?

When you choose they should attend you? . . .

Mrs Bate joins me in all respects to Mrs Garrick . . .

N.B. She is the most extraordinary Quick study I ever heard of.

And now Sarah's Sid got into the act with a somewhat servile letter to the go-between, Bate:

Revd Sir,

Your comm. safe to hand this morning. I confess I was under some concern not hearing from you sooner . . .

I am very agreeable Mrs Siddons shall be brought to bed in the country and therefore shall continue here at Gloucester till she is able to remove to London meanwhile hope to be favoured by your correspondence with any advice you shall please to offer, or instructions Mr Garrick shall please to send me. Be so good, Sir, as to present my most respectful compliments to him, and to assure him he has conferred an eternal obligation on me by his offer of the Cash but I hope I shall not have occasion to trouble him for the pains you have taken and the Services done me I shall ever retain the most grateful sense, and am, with Mrs Siddons' respects, your very hum. sert.

Wm. Siddons

Whereupon Garrick wrote to Sarah's Sid a letter full of thought for her condition.

This is one of the first letters I have written since my recovery from a Severe fit of gravel, which rendered me incapable of any business—As I am now much better, I flatter myself that a letter from me will not be disagreeable—I wish to know how Mrs Siddons is? . . . I beg that she will not make herself uneasy about coming (to London) till she will run no risk by the journey. If in the meantime you find it convenient to have any pecuniary Assistance from Me I shall give it You with Great Pleasure. Let me once more intreat that Mrs Siddons may have No Cares about me to disturb her, and that she may not be hurried to the least prejudice of her health.

Then, in a postscript, Garrick added: "My hand shakes with weakness but I hope you will understand the Scrawl."

This Garrick followed with another considerate letter:

Whenever You please to Draw upon Me for the fifteen pounds I shall pay it immediately—I am glad to hear that Mrs Siddons is so Well and Expect you will give me Notice when she is worse and better . . .

When Sarah's time came, she was appropriately enough on-stage, as her mother had been before her, and for that matter no doubt her Sainted Grandmother, too. One can imagine with what relief Garrick wrote again to Sid:

I wish you joy of Mrs Siddons' safe Delivery and I hope she continues well . . . And now about your coming to London . . . let me Desire you to give me the earliest Notice when you and Mrs Siddons can be here . . .

And with what pride Sid replied:

From my former accounts for Mrs Siddons' Time you'll be surprised when I tell you she is brought to bed. She was

[69]

unexpectedly taken ill when performing on the stage and produced me a fine girl. They are both, thank heaven, likely to do well.

To this Sid added a P.S.:

I have just had the pleasure of seeing Mr Dinwiddie whom you commissioned to supply me with the CASH. He told me I might have any sum I had occasion for so have made bold to take Twenty Pounds which I hope will meet your approbation.

⊰ Chapter 12 ⊱

THREE profusely rouged ladies were sitting before a skimpy fire in theatrical digs not far from the Lane. They were discussing, none too kindly, the Great Garrick and his new rustic Venus.

For Mrs Siddons had come to town and was, though outwardly calm, in a permanent inward panic. When she was with her children, little Henry and baby Sarah, something less than two months old, she was tormented by the thought that she should have been preparing her Portia, and when she was rehearsing she was well-nigh rent in two because she was not with her children; and this in spite of the vigilance of Nannie Noakes. That one had taken her to task firmly. "All this blether about two dear little souls who have Me to look to, just as you did before them!"

"Oh Betsy, dear Betsy, I know, I know. But Baby Sarah did not recognise me when you brought her to my dressing-room today. I swear to the Heavens she did not—she would not suckle my milk."

"Babes have moods like the rest of us," said Nannie Noakes. "And to my mind you're nobbut a babe yourself, Sairey."

"I am a Married Woman and," there was a sob in her voice, "twice a Mother," said Sarah with a pathetic attempt at matronly dignity. Child-bearing had left her weak.

"Then pick up yonder Henry in the coal-scuttle, as usual, and change his nappy while I attend to my Ladybird, poor little thing."

"But my Trial Scene," cried the poor wretched Sarah Siddons. Mr Dibdin was right: Life was nothing but a roisterous tug-o'-war.

Poor youthfully sensitive Mrs Siddons. Compelled to travel by Public Conveyance from familiar and friendly Cheltenham to an unknown London, with the terrors of the Trial at the Lane ahead; and this before she had fully recovered from the agony and weakness of childbirth. Trundling and bumping along rut-ridden country roads in a Public Conveyance, which swung perilously at every wind of the lanes so as to render the stoutest-hearted party coach-sick, proved hard and comfortless to the female frame. She was cooped close with a pack of disapproving strangers and a decidedly crochety, because alarmed, Nannie Noakes, with her dear Sid compelled to ride outside, sharing the Box with the coachman on this snow-flaked December journey that was certain to land him in the Metropolis with streaming eyes and nose. And those two angels, her very young children, little Henry—a tender two-year-old and sick all over an elegant but acid Lady in a blue velvet cloak—and the babe, Sally, to be suckled in full view of the inquisitive passengers, which fascinated the males and shocked the females just as though they themselves would not pay toll in their turn to Dame Nature in the self-same way. Not, then, the kind of journeying to be undertaken lightly.

And what if Mr Garrick were to find her talents at low ebb, her suitability to perform before a sophisticated audience lacking?

What if he were to send her back, Babes and baggage? What if her scant breath—a flaw left over from her difficult delivery—prevented her from giving her Trial Scene due weight and importance? Or if her worn costumes were too simple? Or if her trim figure and taking looks were gone for ever—for ever!

But the three ladies, gossiping over Tay and muffins in the theatrical lodgings they shared, knew nothing of Mrs Siddons' physical weakness, nor of her maternal stress. They saw her only in her perilous calm in which she sought to restore her courage and her spirits—a calm all too easily broken these days—and cared nothing for the shadows beneath her eyes. To Mrs Abingdon, Mrs Yates and Miss Young, who were soon to be joined by Mrs Clive, she was the Threat.

It was all very fine for Mr Garrick to stand, no doubt, on tiptoe, to hiss in the ear of Posterity that Mrs Abingdon, the ring-leader of this Witches' brew, was below the thought of any man or woman, and that she was as silly as she was false and treacherous, but did he say this to her face? Was it her fault that, with the aid of high heels, like Mrs Prichard's Lady when she took the Daggers from her strongly reluctant stage-spouse, Mrs Abingdon towered over Wee Davey and he was painfully aware of it? And since when had one insecure player spoken the truth about another?

We breed, we happy breed, removed by the centuries from the charmingly faded passions of Sarah Siddons' days, might even summon up some kind of forgiveness for Mrs Abingdon, pitched out of the dregs of The Town as she had been; living for years as a Tavern Girl. Well may it seem to us that the cupidity and obscenity of the first Lady Teazle were quite touching when one sensed them underlying the quiet airs she, like Peg Woffington, had somehow come by in a harsh school, and never more so than when all the Milliners of Dublin's fair city were displaying "the Abingdon Cap" in their shop-windows.

Ever since she had stepped from the buskins into the breeches of Scrubb in *The Beaux Stratagem* she had been above herself. That she had not as yet laid hands on the skull-and-sable business of Hamlet did not mean that her heavily be-ringed, yet oft grimy hands were not capable of pouncing on The Dane. It would be a change, she vowed, and half-meant it. In the matter of kittenish humour and high spirits la Abingdon considered herself a *non-pareil*.

"And those draggle-tail feathers in her bonnets or rather bonnet, I should have said, for I have long suspected the lady has but one," declared the Queen of Headgear. It was perfectly clear to Mrs Yates and Miss Young that la Abingdon was speaking of Sarah Siddons.

"And her boots," said Mrs Yates—she with the classical profile of the Antique World, discarding for the afternoon all its calm and much of its monotony—one could not be oneself and say what one really meant while maintaining the Classical Profile. "Did ever you see such clumsy clod-hoppers?"

"I'd as soon be seen in clogs," said Miss Young. "And when she is impassioned . . ."

"When is she not?" Mrs Yates asked the ceiling. (Angelica Kauffmann? Naturally.)

"The faces she pulls!" Miss Young pulled a sour face to illustrate. "And I have heard from a very clever person, too, that in rehearsing a tragedy, there is not the slightest occasion to speak in a dismal voice, or to put on a long, melancholy face, so long as you assume it at night."

"That, she will do," Mrs Yates dug her nose in the air.

"And her vowels," Miss Young marvelled.

"Those vowels she has brought with her from the Midlands!" In the matter of criticising a fellow artiste Mrs Abingdon was not to be left out. "Veering towards Wales," she suggested.

"Llandudno," Miss Young clinched it.

"I do not dislike the slut, but there is no doubt at all that she lowers the *Ton*. French, my dears." Mrs Abingdon patted her curls complacently at this display of sophistication.

"La! Let us give her the Treatment," said Mrs Yates.

Miss Young clapped her hands. "At her *début*," she said.

About Miss Young. Was not Mr Leigh Hunt, the critic, to call this young lady the most admirable Mrs Malaprop the Lane had seen when she was no longer young? And had not the author of *Wild Oats* praised her Lady Amaranth? In fact, though by general consent she was "above middle height" and her manner could be "commanding", we are warned that her face was "not handsome" poor spinster, for this was before Mr Pope (No Relation), a gourmand, proposed. But power, of a florid sort, she had. After her first performance at Drury Lane her salary was raised to three pounds, and by the end of her first season, to five pounds, and this, we are told, was "unsolicited". She was a particular favourite of Garrick and played Cordelia to his last Lear, on the last night but one of his appearing on the stage, when he led her into the green-room and fetched a deep, deep sigh:

"Oh Bess! This is the last time of my being your Father! You must now look out for someone else to adopt you."

"Then, Sir," said she falling upon her knees, "pray give me a Father's blessing."

"God bless you — God bless them all."

Miss Young was in the habit of relating this with evident pleasure and rarely without tears.

These three ladies, hags before their time, were the hard core of the operation. But before they had reduced the reputation of Sarah Siddons to the last tatter a commotion arose in the vestibule — Kitty Clive had arrived back at her lodgings from an expedition to the shops. There was a vigorous kicking at the parlour door.

"Open up? Let me in! Aid me!" For Mrs Clive's hands were full and her considerable person almost obscured behind the bundles and boxes without which a fashionable actress could not be called a fashionable actress. Finally the door yielded and Mrs Clive was able to plump herself on the *chaise-longue* amid a sea of purchases which caused it to creak and squeak as though complaining of the burden. "Well, you three Witches, whose reputation have you consigned to the cauldron along of the eyes of newts and toes of frogs?" she enquired with her customary good humour.

"You're late," snapped Mrs Abingdon, without hers.

Mrs Clive kicked off her shoes and set about rubbing the blood back into her toes. "Fie how me back aches! What a jaunce have I had!"

She turned to Miss Young. "Come love! Come Lady-Bird! Help me to enlarge my tight lacing. We cannot all be willowy Goddesses," she observed with some truth as she tugged at her decolletage to shepherd her goodly breasts into their most plentiful position.

"After all," she addressed herself to Miss Young's less luxuriant figure, "after all, you are *Younger* than I!" And she emitted a peal of laughter at her own wit and flung her legs into the air, freely exhibiting her cerise stockings. For in the words of Mr Pope—the Poet not the Husband:

> Here liv'd the laughter-loving Dame
> A Matchless actress, Clive her name—

that same jovial, ugly, laughter-loving Kitty Clive who, by her bustle and humour, had saved many a Fifth Act that had never got itself round to being rehearsed. Indeed had not Dr Johnson sent her spinning down to Posterity;

"She was a better Romp than any I saw in Nature."

And was not the gnarled old Doctor borne out by the lines:

First giggling, plotting Chamber maids arrive
Hoydens and Romps led on by General Clive,
In spite of outward blemishes she shone
For Humour famed, and humour all her own.

And as for Tate Wilkinson, the Strolling Patentee, he has set
it down that "Mrs Clive was a mixture of combustion, for she is
passionate, cross, vulgar, yet sensible — a very sensible woman".
Even though Mr James Boaden, at present acting as tutor to the
Vicar of Wakefield's family settled in Auburn, loveliest village of
the Plain, was later to chide, "Mrs Clive never mastered the
elements of language and spells most audaciously."

With such an array of talent and temperament lined up against
her, small wonder Sarah Siddons inwardly quailed.

"The tay has grown quite cool. Shall I brew some fresh?"

"Nay, my dear," Kitty Clive drew out the pins in her high-
crowned, befeathered and beribboned and rose-dotted and
giddily inclined hat, and tossed it on the floor beside her.
Straight away her hair came down in a scarlet shower.

"A can of chocolate then? I will make it myself," volunteered
Mrs Yates.

"Bad for the complexion, but good to the taste," said Mrs
Clive. "La! my dear, do not displace yourself," she added,
making no feint to displace herself.

But Mrs Yates had already sailed off into regions below.

"Did you observe Mrs Yates' Lady Teazle last night?" asked
Mrs Abingdon, taking the opportunity of Mrs Yates' absence to
switch enmities for a time. Kitty Clive shook the scarlet shower.

"I fear," said Miss Young falsely, "she made her something
of a romp."

"Too much stomping about and too much flumping about,"
said Mrs Clive in a phrase that was to become famous. She sniffed.

Chapter 13

ALL, then, was not well with Mrs Siddons even though Garrick honoured his promise of five pounds a week, which must have seemed a mint of money. She who was accustomed, in Dr Johnson's phrase, to towering in the full confidence of twenty-one, looked on the empty vast spaces of the Theatre Royal, Drury Lane, during rehearsals and trembled. Her fears were sapping her and indeed laying her low. Betsy, for the sixth time at least, assured her that "Doctor Theatre" would restore her once her opening night was actually on the way. "Put your trust in the Lord, and Doctor Theatre — Shakespeare," Betsy repeated. The impulsive Sarah Siddons was forced to hang on to the arms of her carver's chair to stop herself from picking up the pile of plates set before her and hurling them at her one-time Nannie (and sprigged china, so expensive). And what would her handsome little son and her rose-petal daughter do then, she asked herself wildly?

Garrick had chosen Portia from the list of characters she had submitted as suitable to her London début and had cast Tom King for her Shylock, a strange choice, of whom that taster of the actors of his day, mild little Mr Lamb, had written, "His acting left a taste on the palate sharp and sweet like quince; with an old, hard, rough withered face, like a john-apple, puckered up into a thousand wrinkles."

A sympathetic Shylock, then. Those three freshly painted Caskets! The quality of Mercy—at last! What could be lacking for a triumph? And the Wee God Garrick there to crown it by publicly presenting his new leading lady with the aquamarine glass and pinchbeck locket that he himself wore in the Closet Scene in Hamlet for "Look now upon this picture". It also did service for "Some rich jewel" with which he would toy when playing Malvolio in all the glory of cross-garters. He would of course take care to remember to re-possess himself of it in the wings after Curtain-fall. What could go wrong with such a début? And hindsight answers, "Pretty well everything."

✣ Chapter 14 ✣

THE wings were full on the evening of Sarah Siddons' début at Drury Lane. It seemed to her alarmed senses that half London and the whole of Garrick's company had squeezed themselves in, and all of them viewing her with cold eyes and, as the evening wore on, her young strength failed her. Her voice could not be heard beyond the third row of seats; the carefully acquired vowels she had learned at Guy's Cliffe had deserted her. "Louder—speak louder," mouthed her Shylock. "More voice." And Sarah, accustomed to the ladies in provincial audiences who were wont to swoon dead away at her very entrance, even before she started Giving, and the stronger sex who blew on their noses as though to trumpet away the tears that brimmed their eyes, quailed before the coldness of the House. She did not stalk her stage in the accepted manner. Rather, she tottered on and tottered off.

In the wings Mrs Abingdon, Mrs Yates and Miss Young, a sour Greek Chorus, were stationed. Kitty Clive had found something better to do with an Admiral of the Line; and the Greek Chorus could be heard with sufficient clarity each time the débutante came to a big moment. Not that Portia was a part in which to tear a passion to shreds.

"Is she intoxicated?" asked Mrs Abingdon.

"Probably—though hardly on praise," said Mrs Yates.

Almost they might have been Kezia and Salubria back in the dear old afternoons in Farmer Hassock's Barn—"the Bull has been removed to Farthermost Field."

"And her arms when not sawing the air," Miss Young strove to illustrate, "are quite commonplace."

"You mean downright common," said Mrs Abingdon loudly.

"And whoever played Portia in a second-hand salmon-coloured sacque?" Miss Young asked of the flies.

Actually the offending garment had been fished out of Madam Kemble's stock wardrobe basket (or would do for Sigismunda and equally for Ariadne—*The Rival Sisters*) to the envy of Kezia Quicktobed and Salubria Golightly.

Poor sensitive timorous Sarah. Her Mama was not at hand to comfort, support and give her courage from her own lion's share. Broad actress Madam Kemble may have been, but never given to under-statement in the face of her audience, rough and rowdy though they may have waxed. Indeed, as Sarah knew full well, she was at this moment giving her Gertrude at Chipping Camden and had her bejewelled hands full with problems of her own.

But Sarah, not yet recovered from bearing the baby, exhausted, barn-sick and, for the first and last period in her career, inaudible, called upon her Sainted Grandmother just as her mother had done before her.

What more humiliation could lie ahead?

There was a rumble of thunder for all the world as though the Thane of Cawdor were approaching, and a Voice from far above the rooftops of Covent Garden, far, far, far above the moon and stars, spoke in her heart: "Plenty," it predicted. "Doctor Theatre, forsooth!"

If her fellow players did not approve, neither did the Metropolitan Press. Forewarned by the Play Bills (which announced her not by name but as "Portia, a young Lady—being her first appearance") they reported that she spoke hoarsely and was inaudible. There was a vulgarity in her tones. She was advised to throw more fire and spirit into her performance. She, la Siddons, whose power and passion could drive an audience nigh to fits! But they praised her full figure.

Sarah would willingly have departed there and then, preferably by means of a hole in the floor quite unrelated to the stage trap-door. But her Sid insisted she should soldier the season out, and soldier on she did for contracts were contracts even to actors and Sid was determined that Sarah should honour hers, "in case—for you never know". Her next appearance was in *As You Like It* in which her Rosalind disappointed her public too, and particularly those Beaux accoutred with quizzing glass. Even gentle Fanny Burney, writing to her friend Sophia Western, suggested in her impeccable use of words:

> The playful scintillation of colloquial wit which most strongly mark that character suit not the dignity of the Siddonian form and countenance. Her dress was injudicious—an ambiguous vestment that seemed neither male nor female . . .

and the able critic and owner of *The Sun News Sheet*, John Taylor, went into detail:

> . . . Her walk, or rather *strut* on the stage, were those of Lady Macbeth or Belvidera and not of the volatile, sprightly Rosalind . . . a quaint sinking of her voice rendered her inaudible; and the shake and declination of her head were

the only indications of gaiety and humour . . . her dress was the most unaccountable we have ever witnessed upon the stage. It was not that of either man or woman. Her Hussar boots with a gardener's apron and petticoat behind gave her a most equivocal appearance which rendered Orlando's stupidity astonishing . . . she could not appear to less advantage in any other habiliment whatever.

After this came Ben Jonson's *Epicene*, a battle which Sarah failed to win. Then she played right into an ambush in *The Blackamoor Washed White.**

But came the dawn with no brightening of the Fleet Street sky: "All played well except Mrs Siddons," reported *The Morning Chronicle*, "who, having no comedy in her Nature, rendered that ridiculous which the author intended to be pleasant."

And so on to Garrick's own favourite play, *Richard the Third*, in which her Lady Anne received but one critique: "Lamentable."

Not, then, a handsome Press. Sarah Siddons finished it, but that first Drury Lane season started a hardening process in her nature.

It was, no doubt, something in the arrangement of the stars that in 1776 England lost America; and Mrs Siddons, Drury Lane. It is certain that His Majesty felt the loss less keenly than Sarah Siddons. She could not, mid-season, hope to join a circuit and to keep her Sid and "my poor Babes". She had to scratch out some one-week or two-week provincial engagements like a moulting hen. She was miserably conscious of her London failure, and knew that it would be set down to her discredit in all the towns she toured. And though when she left the Lane in June it was said by Garrick to be but until the next season, she

* A suitable subject for the Royal Court Theatre?

should not have been surprised when Garrick's successors, the new Management of the establishment who, after his retirement, were headed by Thomas Sheridan, wrote to break the news to her of the Termination of her Engagement.

Small wonder that, some years later, when she learned that Sheridan had considered Garrick's *Richard the Third* insufficiently awe-full, she was startled into exclaiming in tones of strong disbelief: "Good God! What could be more terrible!" Could the great little man have heard of the remark? Could he have misunderstood it, if room for misunderstanding were in truth there?

Be that as it may, there was no misunderstanding in *l'affaire Cervetto*.

Ever since the fashionable painter Zoffany had painted him with perceptive accuracy, Cervetto was generally held to be the leading cellist of his age. When he came to England from Venice and joined the orchestra at Drury Lane Theatre, it was said to be a considerable coup for that establishment, in spite of a cherry-nosed claque in the gallery, no doubt employed by rival and probably British cellists, shouting "Play up, Nosey": though, in the matter of long noses, his came second to that of Sarah Siddons, whose nose was to be the despair of painters yet to come. He annoyed Garrick, however, by yawning loudly during his performance of Richard Crookback. Garrick glared. Sarah Siddons turned her back to hide her amusement. But not before Garrick had switched glares and caught his Lady Anne smiling. And though Cervetto sent round a note saying that that he always yawned when "very mush please", the incident was not forgotten and perhaps never forgiven.

So Mrs Siddons departed on her touring, always accompanied by the ruffled and easily put out Sid, with her two children wailing and trailing after her and the muttering Nannie Noakes, from Brecon to Bristol, from Bristol to Birmingham, Birmingham to Liverpool, Liverpool to Manchester, from Manchester to

York and back to Birmingham again. She swayed and bumped
nd dreaded the morrow.

At her very first Birmingham appearance, weak and exhausted,
Sarah was confronted by an unruly gallery: "She motions
nicely but she cannot shout out loud," was the sum total of the
opinion of the Gods of the New Theatre, who certainly could
and, to prove it, did—loud and long.

One good gallery-goer in the Provinces, on the appearance of
Sarah Siddons as Isabella in *The Fatal Marriage*, rose to his
feet in beer-begotten anger.

"Drat the girl!" he exclaimed, "Always getting into trouble!"

For a year and a half after leaving Drury Lane, Mrs Siddons
could hardly bring herself to name the place without a shudder
that seemed to come from her soul. "I was said to be hastening
to a decline." And from that moment on, Sarah was prone to
look upon her own enemies as those of the Lord—the more so
as the hardening of her warm young nature set in firmly.

It was at Birmingham that the blow fell. Sid had written to
Garrick to ask him to use his influence, now that he was retiring
from Management, upon the new Establishment at Drury Lane
to re-engage his wife for the following season: a foolish letter
in which he tried to excuse the inexcusable.

Sarah, late for breakfast, having first given her Little Rosebud
Princess hers, descended to the public Breakfast Room at the
Inn to find her Sid in a state of shock.

"My love, bad news from London," he said, and the sheet of
paper in his hand shook.

"Give me the letter," she commanded, with all the firmness
of purpose of a future Lady Macbeth.

"And all I asked was three pounds a week for you and two
for me, that we should not disgrace the Acting Profession!"
he mourned.

Sarah Siddons read on. Sid was too soft. She dug her chin

in the air. It was the Kemble chin. "I shall deal with this matter myself," she said, with the decision that was to become second nature to her before long.

Half a century later she was to record a note for her biographer to clear her fame and bring to light the jealousies and prejudices her career had to overcome in its climb — which, at this stage, resembled more a clamber — to the heights. To put her reverse into her own words, which were also those of Hamlet, or very nearly:

Oh, good James Boaden, what a wounded name
Things standing thus unknown shall leave behind me!

And even fifty years on, she could not forbear from finishing the passage:

If thou should ever hold me in thy heart,
Absent thee from felicity a while,
And in this harsh world draw thy breath in pain
To tell my story.

For were not these the poor boy's very words? And might she not have played her entire repertory of Elsinore characters — Ophelia, Gertrude, the Player Queen, the Lord Hamlet, in a kind of one-man — well, one-woman then — show?

When the London season was over [she jotted down — if "jotting" be the word to apply to the freshly-sharpened quill pen, the pointed hand-writing, the careful sanding and the firm sealing], I made an engagement at Bir^m for the ensuing Summer, little doubting of my return to Drury Lane for the next Winter . . .

To my utter astonishment and dismay I rec^d an official letter from the Prompter of Drury Lane [he who was to become in the course of time her brother jolly John Philip

[86]

Kemble's Pa-in-law], acquainting me that my services were no longer necessary. Who can conceive the size of this cruel disappointment (that little rogue Harry is clattering to such a degree I scarce know what I am about) this dreadful reverse of all my ambitious hopes in which, too, was involved the subsistence of two helpless infants! It was very near destroying me . . . and preyed upon my health, and for a year and a half.

For the sake of my poor babies, however, I exerted myself to shake off my Despondency and my endeavours were crowned with success . . .

Chapter 15

DRAT the ink blot!

In York Mrs Siddons carried all before her, a pleasing change from Drury Lane, both in Tragedy, as might have been expected, and Comedy, which in other cities had seemed a little tarnished by the fact that, notable as she was for her unconscious humour, she had no hint of it about herself, and it is certain that she was no *soubrette*—perish the thought! More, she put a Miss Glassington effortlessly and completely in the shade, and caused a Mrs Hudson to flare up in the face of Mr Tate Wilkinson and sweep out of any enterprise of his for ever.

Across a pinch of Tate Wilkinson's most excellent Irish snuff, for "Tragedy's divinest daughter" loved snuffing, Mrs Siddons and Mr Wilkinson found themselves in complete agreement over the baseness of Garrick *Tyrannos*. Sarah confided —to Wilkinson's delight—that she liked her country excursions and the civilities she met with so well, and thought her treatment in London so cruel and unjust, she never wished to play there again. Indeed Tate Wilkinson was of the firm opinion that Provincial Theatres, and particularly his own, were better than those of the Metropolis.

"The Little Theatre in the Haymarket," as it was called in George the Third's day, would now cut a very contemptible figure in most other towns in England, and was not fit to enter after seeing Bath, Bristol, Liverpool, York ... "Drury Lane, like London Bridge, had been much frittered."

So cosy were these midnight meetings spent *en famille* by Sarah and Sid, Tate Wilkinson and his own good wife that the, at this stage of the Season, Stationary Patentee tried to bribe his Provincial Star with promises of "silks and fine theatrical array" to return to York as a resident luminary as soon as her contractual Strolling was concluded; but she merely responded with a toss of her ostrich feathers (Mistress Madcap in *Excentricity Hall*). There was in particular a silver-foil trimmed, sky-blue satin sacque on a large whaleboned hoop, which he had produced from Wardrobe for her Dulcie in the *Druidess* (or would do for Sabrina in *Comus*, which was played by his company in modern eighteenth-century dress).

Tate Wilkinson was a wily man. Knowing that Sarah much coveted the costume, he decided to use it as a material carrot, as it were, to tempt her to remain in York. He removed the hoop, for Sarah Siddons was one of the earliest of anti-hoop ladies, although he himself was partial to whalebone hoops on his stages. Whaleboned skirts took up so much space on stage that he could dispense with at least three extras in pictorial scenes. He hung the costume on the door, where the flames of the log fire caught the gleaming satin, and where the glinting foil must catch la Siddons' eye.

"I found a beautiful plum-coloured silk today. Mrs Jordan looked on it with some favour, but 'No,' I said, 'No. It is promised to Mrs Siddons—when she returns to us'."

La Siddons tossed her ostrich feathers again. Almost she

[89]

might have been a horse—a fly-bitten, highly irritated horse—
at some *grande funeraille*.

"Promises, promises," she snapped. She recalled her purpose
to mind. She did her best to simper (Mignonette in *Innocence
Violated*). She may have been a thoroughly Modern Woman,
but she was not above dissembling to gain her ends, when a
costume hung in the balance. She gazed with melting eyes at
the dress practically dancing by itself in the firelight. She looked
at Tate Wilkinson, and she melted some more.

"I feel so happy, so inexpressibly happy—except that when I
play Dulcie I do express—when I am wearing that beauteous
costume," she confided to the Company gathered around the
snuff box. "Do I not, Sid?"

Her handsome Sid nodded. It cost him nothing.

"Then I, too, am happy," Tate Wilkinson assured his star,
but thin lips were pressed together. His good wife, who knew
his every nuance—who better?—detected a wariness in him.

"So ridiculously happy!" Sarah laughed her most adorable
laugh. Maybe it was less adorable than Kitty Clive's more
spontaneous laughter, but it was the laugh she had cultivated
in the Mail Coach for her Perdita, to the evident astonishment
of her fellow passengers.

Her Sid looked suddenly less than happy. He, too, could
read signs in his spouse's demeanour. "Well, well, well," he
said. He took a pinch of snuff and hoped for the best.

"And when I am happy my voice rings out to the very last
auditor in the Gods, does it not, my love?"

Sid's nose twitched, his eyes watered. "Atchoo! Atishoo!"
was all he could get out.

Fortunately Sarah had left him no time to add to it, but had
gone ringingly on to her favourite topic of the month.

"I declare," she declared, throwing up one arm as though
challenging the skies (*The Grecian Daughter*). This was unwise.
A chill ran up and down her spine, and she was aware of pins

and needles in her left foot. (Her Sainted Grandma at it again?) "I declare that the punctuation of applause not only invigorates my whole system, but the space of time it occasions assists the breath and nerve." She thrice drew a deep breath and expelled it.

Tate Wilkinson, too, was anxious not to commit himself. "Indeed," he said.

"On the other hand, when I am not happy . . ." Sarah Siddons refrained from finishing what was, if not an outright threat, at least a very broad hint.

"Atishoo!" It was her Sid, but Sarah had no intention of allowing anyone to steal her scene. She coughed. That cough would have done for *La Dame aux Camélias*, had the immortal play been written. It had not.

Tate Wilkinson, who was wily in his ways with women, allowed the paroxysm of coughing to die away and a prolonged silence to take its place, in the hope that the subject might languish and die a gentle death. It did not. He had under-estimated his Sarah. She returned to the attack. Once again she melted.

"See how the silver foil glistens in the candlelight and the satin glows in the firelight! Ah!" she sighed. "And how softly, how caressingly—" her voice made love to the word—"the folds fall without the stiffness and lack of feminity of those unpleasing whalebone hoops. I know what you are about to say." She raised her hand to hush him. "You are about to remind me that Queen Charlotte herself wears hoops."

"She holds that they lend an Appearance of Consequence," said the loyal Mrs Tate Wilkinson.

"Quite so." Tate Wilkinson's voice, in spite of his smile, held the wintry dryness of a cracker.

"But," Sarah ignored the smile on the face of the tiger, "how far from Queenly our beloved Queen can be if one catches her in an off moment—and we all have them! Why, any capable actress playing a Queen making an entrance with a crown is far more Queenly than a Queen. Not Mrs Hudson, perhaps, but that Lady is so ungainly. I," she said with unusual confidence, "am not, am I, my love?"

"You, my dear, are every inch a Queen when you are wearing nothing at all," said the wretched Sid.

Mrs Siddons gave him what was to be known as one of her looks before, to hide her natural embarrassment, she bent over the poker and administered so shrewd a blow at the logs that the sparks flew.

"Pretty as it is, that costume has done good service in our company, Husband," pointed out the compassionate Mrs Tate.

"But it would bring back so many happy memories of my Grecian Daughter and dear, dear York!" Mrs Siddons was right back to cooing again. "Why, Sir," she turned to Tate, "you yourself have praised my elegance in it and made flattering comments about my Pictorial Attitudes when I fall and die upon the stage—please allow me to take it with me."

"I have a better idea," Tate Wilkinson said. "It is yours." Mrs Siddons lent forward. "Yours to wear whenever you play in my Company."

He passed her his golden snuff box: it had been a gift from the great little Garrick. Its Recipient had never recovered from his shock of displeasure when he found that the great little man had been little enough to stoop to pettiness. The precious metal was not precious at all. Tate Wilkinson's pawnbroker had broken the news to him one hard Winter when he needed to raise the wind.

"Snuff, my child?" he offered.

Mrs Siddons snuffed. Never again, she decided, should she stoop to a Woman's Wiles unless, of course, the role demanded it. (Rosalind, *As You.*) Tomorrow she would be herself—or what herself was henceforth to be. Tomorrow she would see what threats would do for her. From this time on, she would be all Lady Macbeth.

[92]

⊷⊰ Chapter 16 ⊱⊶

So started Sarah Siddons' six and a half years' exile from London, if the Bath of her day, the seasonal resort of high fashion, "the more select London", can so be styled. She had come to it gratefully after a prologue of playing in the smug and vulgar provinces, where people paid their cash and imagined they knew what was what and appearing at the larger but dull country towns, a prologue by no means devoid of incident.

Crude as was the rouge, the white chalk shaded by dust or soot, it became her habit to make-up and to don her usually weighty costume at the Inn at which she was lodged, that not one moment of her playing with her little roguish Prince and her infant Princess be lost to their adoring Mama; and, thus bedizened and attired, take to her rather large feet and run through the streets, publicly mouthing what lines she could remember without a hurried refresher course in the Sides.

It was at Brecon that, detained by some sweet domesticity, she had left it sadly late to set out for the Theatre where she was about to give her Benefit version of Ophelia in her Mad

Scene. She ran down the street, her hair wild and dishevelled, all threaded through with simulated river weeds and wild flowers, publicly mouthing her words and breaking into snatches of song, robbed of their bawdiness by her innocent panic. She would be late. Oh, why had she not heeded Gypsy Noakes' warning?

Mrs Siddons pounded on, no respectable Sabine Woman, fleeing from rape, as fleet as she.

A small girl not five years of age, Jemimah Blish by name, gazed at the leaping lady with naive wonderment. "Ma!" she piped, "why is that untidy lady talking to herself?"

"Hush, my Princess." (Princesses were all the fashion—when have they not been—had not the Queen a litterful of her own?) "That is the London actress Mrs Siddons emerging from one of her Perilous Calms."

"They say the Owl is the Baker's Daughter," chanted Sarah Siddons. "Puff, puff."

"Why, Sister, I've never heard say Mrs Siddons could sing," exclaimed Jemimah's Aunt.

A human bean-stalk with steel rimmed spectacles, who had been lingering to take in the fleeting Siddonian Vision, raised his hat and addressed the little group of country cousins. He was, of course, James Boaden. Fortunately he was passing through Brecon on his way to tutor Tom Jones; Poor Mr Fielding could do nothing with the lad! "Ladies, it is not Mrs Siddons who sings mad songs. It is—" he paused for effect— "Ophelia," he breathed.

At Liverpool Sarah Siddons once again essayed the Gloomy Dane, but of course at this stage of her career she was not so much an inky Male Hamlet as an Ophelia in buskins, wrapped modestly in a great black woollen shawl, which garment successfully hid her nether limbs, thus defeating both her characterisation and any peep-show Tom in sight.

It was in Manchester that Sarah was to meet Elizabeth

Inchbald, an actress at that point, subsequently a writer, who was to bear a strong influence on her life. Her brother, Jolly John Philip Kemble, all thoughts of priesthood thrown over his shoulder, broke away to join the Siddons' *équipe*—not, as well might be imagined, without a deal of family fracas, mainly from that mild and (give a genuflexion, take a genuflexion) devout Roman Catholic, Papa Roger Kemble, and a dutiful rather than devout "Your father is right" from that stout Protestant spouse, Madam Kemble, and an amount of dissenting thunder from above, unusual for the time of year.

It may be imagined that towns, to Mrs Siddons on tour, became so many agonies to be endured in their Theatres or at their Inns, with the children fretful and Nannie Noakes growing no younger as she grumbled on.

In Leeds, where Sarah had played for three nights, she found herself obliged to "skim away to York, not knowing what was to play that night". When she arrived there, the part fixed on the Playbill was not the part for which the carrier had brought the dresses and properties. But at twenty-two our Sarah was too desperate, too tired, or just too downy a bird to make any fuss herself. Using that sudden drop from the lofty to the severely practical which was later to become a lifeline to her, her instant reaction in this crisis was, "I put my confidence in God and left it to Mr Wilkinson to make such changes in the bill as were convenient." A town or two later, there was this scribble sent post-haste to a friend.

"I am sitting in a little dark room in a little wretched Inn in a little poking village at the end of a whole day's journey over bogs and stones in a rattling coach, with another day's journey in front of me."

. . . Poor Mrs Siddons—hardly time for a caesura!

At length, Bath, there also to play pendulum-wise, at Bristol's beautiful little Theatre Royal, built to bear green and gilded witness to the high Georgian drama to this very day.

Here, most of her time must have been spent in the Mail Coach between these two romantic houses of culture; endeavouring to con recalcitrant lines before the marvelling or highfalutin' fellow passengers, and to be bumped, bumped, bumped and swung, swung between the two scenes of her labours, thorough bush, thorough briar, as she herself expressed it—the Immortal Bard had, of course, expressed it before her—through bogs and through mud, over ruts and into potholes, there to Give and to return in the small hours of the morning.

No wonder that, years later, she was to tell the by then scholarly, red-nosed, blinking and stooping James Boaden that oft-times she would still be up and studying a part at three or four in the morning, at which hour a newly-awakened Nannie Noakes would bear down upon the marital chamber and carry the candle-end away.

᭧ Chapter 17 ᭨

IT is to Mrs Inchbald and her diary that we are indebted for an account of Sarah's entrance into Bath, that Fateful City, so calm to the outward eye, but to Sarah Siddons, Sally her Rosebud Princess and the yet unborn Maria, a place of doom indeed:

"I rose at three in the morning and left Manchester in a post-chaise with Mrs Siddons and her maid." (Could Betsy have abandoned her charges? And echo answers, "Most unlikely.") We can imagine that scene around a stout table groaning under a veritable bouquet of good savours. "After which, on to Birmingham, Mr Inchbald on horseback. Mr Kemble was taken in to the chaise by the ladies; till very late in life he was an indifferent horseman."

And horsemanship was not the only thing Jolly John Philip was unskilled in, as yet. He was nineteen. He was handsome, and the gloom that was to be the reason for his soubriquet in these pages had not yet set in. He was, he assured himself,

D   [97]

madly in love with tall, blonde, divine Elizabeth Inchbald, who was quite evidently bored with her possibly worthy, definitely dull, elderly husband. John Philip could not, in the circumstances, take the divine Elizabeth home to meet his parents. Home was so peripatetic. But he could do the next best thing. He could introduce her to his sister Sarah. He did.

The friendship, then, between the Siddons and the Inchbalds burgeoned. Indeed, on one of the gaps between engagements, it had flowered into a *villeggiatura*, a shared holiday on the Yorkshire moors of which Mrs Inchbald leaves a domestic impression in her diary of Mrs Siddons doing the family washing and singing gaily the while, and another of Sarah's feeding her Rosebud Princess between making a hearty meal of a large basin of bread and milk herself. Oh the delights of love and Burgundy.

But this was on holiday. At Bath and Bristol, Life had become an altogether more serious affair once more, and it soon became her custom to immerse herself in a part on journeys, in time borrowed from refreshing her memory for the evening's plays; for time is expandable to those who most need to know how best to use it.

Once more she determined to study Lady Macbeth, in spite of her jigsaw of performances and rehearsals at Bath and Bristol. This time she would master the Lady fully and seriously.

For an earlier lesson learned in panic and anguish was engraved upon the timeless portals of the less than cosy Maison Macbeth. A lesson enforced upon her brash Stroller's confidence when, because she was a quick study and, too, had her trusty Sides to coach her at the last minute. "Abandon slapdash conning, all ye who dare to attempt the Scottish play here." For though the part is short, the import is tremendous. Sarah Siddons shall tell her own story of this lightly-entered into folly. Who better?

It was my custom to study my characters at night, when all

the domestic cares and business of the day were over. On the night preceding that in which I was to appear in the part for the first time, I shut myself up as usual when all the family were retired, and commenced my study of Groach Macbeth. As the character is very short, I thought I should soon accomplish it. Being then only twenty years of age, I believed that little more was necessary than to get the words into my head, for the necessity of discrimination and the development of character, at that time of my life, had scarcely entered into my imagination. I went on with tolerable composure, in the silence of the night (a night I can never forget) till I came to the Assassination, when the horrors of that scene rose to a degree that made it impossible for me to get farther. I snatched up my candle and fled the room in a paroxysm of terror. My dress was of silk and the rustling of it, as I ascended the stairs to go to bed, seemed to my panic-struck fancy like the movement of a spectre pursuing me. At last I reached my chamber, where I found my husband fast asleep (he would be). I clapt my candlestick down upon the table, without the power of putting the candle out, and I threw myself on my bed without daring to stay even to take off my clothes.

At peep of the day I rose to resume my task; but so little did I know of my part when I appeared in it at night, that my shame and confusion cured me of procrastination for the remainder of my life.

So busy was Sarah Siddons in Bath, creating a routine of Appearances and rehearsals and travelling to two towns, twelve miles apart, that took up to three hours in her day, from Bath to Bristol, Bristol to Bath; making time in both, where no time actually existed, for the domesticities, that it was indeed no small mercy that her delightful second daughter, Maria, did not make her bow to the world until the end of the year.

Meanwhile there came another to Bath. The very one who

was to cast a dark shadow into the future, to trouble Sarah and her two adored daughters; the lad with a load of talent, who was to tangle the skeins of their fate. One whom we have met before, a mere child, galloping round a table on his hobby-horse in the fire and candlelight of an Inn. By now in his teens, though in his complete confidence and self-possession he might have been twenty years of age and more, he had had said of him by the painter Hoare that, had he to choose a model for a picture of Christ, he should select the face of young Thomas Lawrence. Nevertheless, the shadow he threw into their three lives was as evil and twisted as the form of Richard the Third, whom the great Edmund Kean was to play with such a vibrant gusto in their own day. In her last years at Bath, Lawrence was to paint Sarah Siddons as Euphrasia in *The Grecian Daughter*, "at the moment when she stabs the tyrant". Heady stuff.

It is fascinating to think of Mrs Siddons, between rehearsal and performance, carried in a chaise to the holy of holies, the Pump Room in Bath, gazing at the Classical Ladies of Mr Josiah Wedgwood whom, but for that plaguey nose of hers, she so strongly resembled.

Of course, wherever she went, be it Bath, be it Bristol, all eyes were upon her. In Bath she fortified her acquaintanceship with the exquisite Duchess of Devonshire, and achieved a lasting, extremely influential friend. She found, too, another lifelong friend in Thomas Sedgewick Whalley D.D., who with a typical eighteenth-century shrugging off of Parish responsibility had removed himself from Lincolnshire to Somerset, where he resided in the winter in Bath and in the summer in a country estate on the outskirts of Bristol. This, the most secular of clerics, and his wife's "dearest friend Mrs Siddons" were on what seem to our laconic ears shamelessly effusive terms. In one letter she assured him that she never went to bed without praying for him and his wife. She wore his hair in a ring, and addressed him, in that spidery and pointed handwriting of hers, as "Your glorious self", "My best, my noblest friend", "My most honoured"; and the Whalleys used to "keep up her strength" with beaten Tent and Eggs and hot-house grapes, and to keep out the cold presented her with magnificent sables—they came in mighty handy for trimmings on the stage robes of Aspasia (*Tamerlane*), The Fine Lady (*Lethe*) and Mary Queen of Scots; also many another character in need of exterior richness.

As to Whalley, he was a particularly minor poet with a way with the ladies who, besides acting as friend and mentor to Mrs Siddons, married three times, and each time married where money was. The last Mrs Whalley, however, had the bad taste to survive him.

Bath society did much to re-affirm young Mrs Siddons' self-confidence. It drew her out until her painful shyness, acquired during her all too brief appearances at Drury Lane, was behind her, and she basked once again on the sunny side of admiration. Conscientiously she started her conning of Lady Macbeth.

So Mrs Siddons, once the hurly-burly of the evening's performance was done, would settle herself to get to grips with the Lady Groach, reading and re-reading the Scottish Tragedy through the small hours until dawn, proverbially rosy-fingered, had touched the creamy Neo-Palladian stucco of the Bath Crescents and Circuses to renewed life; lying down for a snatch of sleep, when she could no longer hold up her head for want of it, then rising to con her scenes again, suiting her lines to her most admired attitudes.

One day—it could have stood for many—she arose two hours earlier than was her habit, descended to the sitting-room of her apartments at Mr Tillings' lodgings on Horse Street Parade, where there was a long looking-glass on the wall, and went through the lines and gestures undisturbed. Undisturbed? Well, that was the object of the exercise. Her Sainted Grandmother, being baulked of her own Lady Macbeth, however, must have had other ideas than that of being supplanted by some chit of a Grand-daughter, even in the Nahum Tate versions of Shakespeare customarily used in the Theatre of her day.

"Wishy-washy," Sarah admitted to herself.

"Namby-pamby," chimed in a gruff gin-roughened voice from afar.

"But," Mrs Siddons comforted herself, "entirely Respectable."

"Tcha!" said a crack in the ceiling. So much, one gathers, for Respectability in the world to come.

That morning found Mrs Siddons moiling and toiling away, when she was disturbed in her studies mid-gesture by the tall, blonde and beautiful Mrs Inchbald.

"Sweet Sarah, you know that I would not interrupt your studies on a mere whim."

Sarah tore her eyes away from the long mirror. "You are a gentle-woman in whom I place an absolute trust," she misquoted, but it was the best she could do without tearing her mind in two.

"Something touching milord John Philip," Mrs Inchbald misquoted too. She was re-studying her Ophelia for her Benefit, easily the most important night of any Thespian's season.

Mrs Siddons essayed an attitude. It did not do. It was replaced by a whirling of arms in stately succession, rather like a sloweddown human windmill, each attitude rejected as soon as reflected.

"Milord John Philip," said Mrs Inchbald, "waxes something importunate." She blushed.

"If 'twere done 'twere well that 'twere done quickly," said Mrs Siddons crisply. "Quickly," she repeated.

But Mrs Inchbald was never a one to take a hint.

"Time and the hour," she observed, for had she not once understudied Mrs Prichard, when that renowned Tragedienne was on the Tate Wilkinson circuit with the Great Garrick—how infirm of purpose Wee Davey had looked beside her when she had stooped from her blonde tallness to grab the dagger from him!—"runs through the roughest day."

Mrs Siddons swung round from the mirror to look reproach-fully at her bosom friend.

"I myself was about to say that," she intimated crossly. She turned back to the long looking-glass, "Now, where was I before I was so rudely interrupted? Ah yes, the haughty Demeanour of one who will brook no contradiction."

Before that quelling look, Mrs Inchbald gave ground.

"No matter," she ceded, "your Elizabeth shall return to supplicate your counsel in most convenient haste beneath some dancing star, sweet Sarah."

"Pray do, sweet Elizabeth—there's sure to be a time for such a word."

Mrs Inchbald took leave of her friend with a merry laugh (*The Unwilling Confidante*) and a "Goodnight, sweet Princess", leaving her to contemplate fresh attitudes.

There was a knock at the sitting-room door, and Sid's anxious head peered round the aperture.

"Your face, my Thane, is as a book in which one reads strange matters. You may advance."

"I'm just off to the Manager's office to ask when we shall receive last week's wage—your three pounds, and," he blushed, "my two pounds."

"Well?" Mrs Siddons sounded anxious. "When?" she demanded.

"Tomorrow," said Sid.

"And tomorrow and tomorrow," said Mrs Siddons, without much hope. She turned back to her long looking-glass. Mr Siddons melted away, but only to be replaced by young Master Lawrence, his painting brush at the ready.

"What bloody man is this?" Mrs Siddons demanded of the ceiling. "The iron tongue of mid-day cannot have tolled twelve!"

"It is nine forty-five a.m. The hour you appointed. I am to crayon your likeness in sepia, in full length as Zara—remember? You promised," said the beautiful lad.

"Not again." Shakespeare's words had deserted Mrs Siddons for the nonce.

"But you promised," protested the boy who had known no boyhood: no period of youth when he was not pursuing the legend of his talent. His lips quivered. Tears were in his eyes. Mrs Siddons could bear this no more than could any fashionable lady in Bath.

"Tomorrow," she promised.

"And tomorrow? And tomorrow," pleaded the lovely lad greedily.

Scarcely had the precocious Lawrence been despatched when a smart rap at the door recalled Mrs Siddons from her gesture.

"Knock, knock, knock," she grumbled with no more pleasure than the Porter in the play she was trying to fit with alternative meanings:

"We? Fail?" She essayed.

"We fail!" she corrected.

The second reading, she decided. The first was much more difficult to achieve, though her Mama, Madam Kemble, simply sailed through the two question marks.

"Knock, knock, knock!"

"Wake Duncan with your knocking!" she called over her shoulder.

But it was only Sid with a face as long as an hour-glass.

"I have come back from the Manager's office," he announced.

"Well?"

"We failed," his voice faltered.

"We? Fail?" said Sarah Siddons, outraged, and without any difficulty at all.

Sid dwindled from the room, only to be succeeded by another bout of knocking.

"Sister! Sister!" It was the voice of Jolly John Philip, hallooing her name to the reverberate hills — *Twelfth Night*, she reminded herself—never do to get the plaguey plays mixed up, like a Stroller. "Enter!" she bade her looking-glass.

In came John Philip, hair ruffled, unshaven and with one sock coming down. A night on the pantiles, the Divine Sarah diagnosed in one swift glare.

"What art thou, so withered and so wild in thy attire?"

"It's the divine Elizabeth."

"I thought it might be."

"She's such a prude!" John Philip stroked his slightly reddened cheek reminiscently.

"Out, damned spot!" commanded Sarah. "*Out*," she emphasised, "Out!" she shouted. She made to hurl her Shakespeare. It had been her Sainted Grandmama's volume, and had seen much similar service. "Hence, horrible shadow, and stand not in the order of your going, but go at once."

It was no good confiding in Sarah. Her brother vanished. She was so plaguily respectable—all Isabella and mighty little Juliet, he defined his sister ruefully.

Mrs Siddons returned to her text and her attitudes. Not five minutes passed before there were disturbing noises off.

Nannie Noakes' voice. "Woe! Woe! Woe!" she chanted, ever closer, ever louder. Not for nothing had she played First Attendant to Madam Kemble's *Mourning Bride*. "Woe! Woe!" she reiterated, like she was heralding the fell sergeant, Death. Automatically Sarah raised a hand to her ear, as though listening and about to protest, "It is the nightingale—caesura—not the lark." She flung open the door, to reveal a squealing purple-faced Nannie Noakes, Henry and Sally, squalling their precious heads off, two kicking and drumming cherubs tucked sturdily under one arm and the new babe under the other.

"Oh hell! What have we here?" There could be no doubt but that Sarah would make a magnificent Lady Macbeth, even though the line was from the *Merchant*.

"Hit's all 'is fault, the little varmint!" H's flying, Betsy miraculously indicated the flailing Master Henry with her chin. "As bad if not worse than his Uncle Johnnie Philip was at his age—rocking his little sister off the see-saw and overbalancing himself after her, and their knees bleeding, and their smocks all dirted up!"

Mrs Siddons' hands flew to her heart. "The multitudinous knees incarnadine," she whispered hoarsely, horror having robbed her of her voice. Distractedly, she rushed away in search of warm water and bandages.

Lady Macbeth could wait. Before everything, she was a Mother!

By the time Mrs Siddons had set her Lady, she had already battled with and won over a fashionable throng, in spite of the indignity of being allotted Siddons Nights on the same evening as the Bath Cotillion, when, according to James Boaden when he was a hunched, scholarly and much respected old man, "everything that could move went to the Lower Rooms". However, even before she had given her Lady Townley on successive Thursdays, throwing in a Lady Restless or so, she had worked her passage to the Tragedies and all was set for the Scottish Play, as it is called in theatre dressing-rooms down to this very day.

It is an indication of Sarah's growing popularity with audiences that the Assembly at the "Dressed Balls" noticeably thinned out in favour of Siddons Nights at the Theatre Royal. By the time the stroke of two rang out in Lady Macbeth's sleep-walking scene, this "Justly Crowned Melpomene", this "Astonishing Tragedienne", this "daughter of a family of Sure Cards", had created her Bath and Bristol public and ventured upon a somewhat bumpy Lady Groach, according to the considered verdict of John Taylor of *The Sun* news-sheets, who recorded along with some detailed praise: "In the taper scene she was defective, her enunciation too confined ... the faces she pulled were horrid, even ugly"—so much for the Long Looking-Glass on the wall at her lodgings. Moreover, it seems that "she appeared in three several dresses"—the first, handsome and neatly elegant; the second, rich and splendid but somewhat pantomimical: and the last, one of the least becoming of any she ever wore upon the stage. (Shades of the infamous Salmon Sacque!) "Lady Macbeth is supposed to be asleep—not *mad*, so that Custom cannot be pleaded as a justification for her appearing in *white* satin.!"

But from this injudicious beginning, The Lady was to become one of Sarah Siddons' most lauded parts, and to come down to history with her, along with Euphrasia, Belvidera and Rosalind, the latter in spite of a dressing-down from the worthy John Taylor.

Lawrence, by now as handsome a lad as ever fell in love with a goddess of beauty, had arrived in Bath shortly after the birth of Sarah's third child Maria, who, wilful in this as in so many other matters, was born during the summer break of 1779, in direct defiance of the Kemble tradition of being born in the wings. We can be sure that her Sainted Great-grandmama, speaking not so much with the tongue of Angels, more in the style of thunder, witches, dragons, and Wagner in a rage, called on the entire winter's night sky to witness to her disapproval, as she sent down snow, hail, and the seven plagues in July. Moreover day jostled night in a manner not shown on the calendar, in a flash of lightning that tore the sky in two, leaving a distinct if momentary impression that Dawn was less a rosy-fingered affair than a gore-dripping talon that wrenched the firmament in twain.

Jake, man of all work at the Theatre Royal, Drury Lane, was affixing a playbill to one of the outer walls. Once he was An Attraction. Once he was a high-wire artist. Once he was as proud and pacey as any of this little lot. "That it should come to this," he muttered. He slapped on the bill, smoothed it, and stood back, his head to one side the better to study the bill he was affixing.

Mrs Siddons (from the Theatre Royal, Bath) will shortly make her appearance at This Theatre in a Capital Character in Tragedy.

Last week it had been Mrs Jordan, and before that Kitty Clive. He shrugged, Jordan, Clive, Siddons, they were all one to him. He picked up his bucket of paste and limped away.

It had taken two years of bracing herself before Mrs Siddons could tear herself away from the adulation of Bath, to face the cruel press and London playgoers again. But since they were offering her an undeniably larger sum than Bath's three pounds a week and Sid's two pounds put together; and since, moreover, she had three little hostages to fortune and a fourth on the way; and not forgetting she owed Nannie Noakes four years' wages, and then, was there not the dawning realisation that Sid was something less than the genius she had thought him in her Strolling days?... Money had become of paramount importance. Besides, she caught herself thinking, that likely lad, Tom Lawrence, had moved his studio to London some months earlier. Oh, infamous thought! She blushed. She was furious with herself for harbouring, however briefly, such idle nonsense — worse, it was ignoble!

⟡ Chapter 18 ⟡

So Mrs Siddons was back at the Lane. But this time, she vowed, she would wear her rue with a difference. This time she had a considerable reputation as a Tragic Actress to uphold her. This time the six years she had windmilled away before long mirrors and treading the uneven boards of West Country playhouses had laid the foundations for a London Triumph. After all what was a Drama Critic but a walking thermometer, there to test the temperature before the paying patrons, about to plunge into the fashionable sea in the auditorium, should totally immerse themselves. Not that Mr Leigh Hunt was ever to lower or bend his own standards, his counsels of perfection, but her achievements in Bath and Bristol had led him and his kind to respect the dragon in the soul of Sarah Siddons. Nevertheless she trembled inwardly.

The play chosen for her return to the Lane was *Isabella or The Fatal Marriage*, a tear-begetter of the first order. Isabella was a role in which she had summoned sufficient tears to furnish forth a waterfall throughout its many revivals in Bath. Moreover,

Mr Sheridan had promised her the vast salary of ten pounds a week—every week—and her eldest child and only son so far, Henry, aged a cheeky eight, was set down to appear with her. And Before Everything, she reminded the room at large, she was A Mother.

"Why are you weeping, Mother, Have you done a fault?" the precocious child piped out.

"There will not be a dry eye in the house," his proud Father promised. He wiped away a tear of his own. So did Sarah. His two little sisters burst into howls, they knew not why. But Betsy Noakes' eyes remained maddeningly dry.

"And who's to teach the blessed angel Turtles from Jays—Shakespeare?" she emphasised, this time with some justification.

A nerve twitched in the proud Father's cheek. He glared at Betsy Noakes.

"Have her tumbled out of the house like an old cheese," he ordered his doe-eyed wife.

Sarah looked at Sid reproachfully. Men were froward, rash and hard to please, as Kate the Shrew observes, but this was ridiculous.

Betsy turned to her eldest nursling: "That man of yours makes me feel older than God's Nurse," she grumbled. "Shakespeare," she claimed with less justification. She lifted the corner of her apron and wiped the infant Roscius' jammy mouth with it. "And who's to larn him manners along with proper grammer?" she demanded. Before everything she was a Nannie, the Family Siddons gathered.

Of course there were the customary hissings and knives-in-the-back from the overtly cooing doves on the distaff side of the company. Sarah herself dwelt upon the awesome preparations in her notes to her biographer, Campbell, half a century later.

For a whole fortnight before that memorable day I suffered from nervous agitation more than can be imagined. No wonder! [She was to toss her dignified headscarf.] For my own fate and that of my little family hung upon it. [Her "little" family, with a fourth child already on its way.] Who can imagine my terror? I fear'd to utter a sound beyond a stage-whisper, but by degrees enthusiasm cheated me into forgetfulness of those fears, and unconsciously I threw out my voice which failed not to be heard in the remotest part of the House by a friend who kindly undertook to ascertain the happy circumstances.

(Who could doubt that this friend was none other than young Boaden, newly returned from Spain where he had been crammer to one of Don Juan's Bastards.)

On the night of October 10th, 1782 (comparable only, her biographers remind us, to the night Garrick shook the town in Richard Crookback in 1741 or when Edmund Kean played Shylock in 1814), la Siddons unleashed just such a torrent of talent and temperament as she usually reserved for her Benefit nights.

What could a poor spiteful actress do but stand in the over-flowing wings on tiptoe to peep at this newly monumental and brilliantly luminous Muse known of old to at least two of that craning company as Sairey Siddons, out of the reach of Kezia Quicktobed and Salubria Golightly, late of Farmer Knightwick's barn—the one at t'other end of yon, now two Walking Ladies, pages, garland-bearers, and "as cast", who had recently been engaged by Thomas Sheridan at Sarah's touchingly humble and generous request, and either or both of whom would gladly have heaved a brick-bat at the glowing, graceful creature who had out-stripped them. She, with her instantly arresting manner, like some torrential flood in motion, bore down upon the stage annihilating all before her.

" 'A trumpet left for Shakespeare's lips to blow' forsooth," sneered Kezia, but she sneered beneath her breath.

"Same old show-off," they agreed. But they agreed in a hiss which might just pass for a whisper, while the audience shrieked when Mrs Siddons shrieked, wept when she wept, swooned when she fell flat on the stage, and palpitated when she palpitated, so persuasive, so imperious were her powers of acting.

So Sarah Siddons, in fact, enjoyed a Renaissance all to herself. Gone for ever was "that trembling Portia, uncertain whereabouts to fix either her eyes or her feet". Give her an archway of whatever dimensions, this time, and she would contrive to fill it. Looking back later in life, when she had entered her seer and yellow years, "I was an honest actress," she said, her humility mixed with deep satisfaction.

Up in his side-box at Drury Lane, Tate Wilkinson had been joined by "the most gentlemanly Richard the Third from London's Tower to Another Part Of The Wood", as Madam Kemble was wont to claim for her husband, though it must be confessed that gentility was hardly one of Crookback's customary qualities. Unfortunately his good lady could not be present herself, for Dickey Suett, the company clown, had a way of getting out of hand on the circuit when Roger Kemble was not there to set the tone, or Mrs Kemble to keep an eye on him, and the sound of his laughter, like a peal of giggles, would rise above itself until it could be heard all over the Theatre Royal, Giggleswick—where else? "Drat Sir Andrew Aguecheek!" she exclaimed unaccountably.

So it was to Roger Kemble alone, or so he thought, that Tate Wilkinson on that weeping, moaning, swooning, fashionable scene, observed: "Were a Wild Indian to ask me what a Queen would look like I would have bade him look at Sarah Siddons."

"My own sentiments precisely," said a bespectacled young man. He had popped uninvited into Tate Wilkinson's side box. Yes, none other than Jimmie Boaden, full of youthful enthusiasm.

Luckily he was not expected to arrive at Lady Teazle's country residence to instil a seemly regard for book-learning in the mind of her wilful little daughter, Samantha, and her new bosom friend and sharer of her Nursery schoolroom, Joseph Surface's small son, until the morrow.

We can safely leave it to Sarah's own words to set the seal on the night's triumph.

On this eventful day my Father . . . accompanied me to my dressing-room . . . and there left me, and I, in what I call one of my desparate tranquillities, completed my dress, to the astonishment of my attendants, without uttering a word, though frequently sighing most profoundly. At length I was called to my fiery trial . . . The awful consciousness that one is the sole object of attention to that immense space, lined as it were with Human Intellect from Top to Bottom and on All Sides round, may perhaps be imagined but cannot be described and never, never to be forgotten . . . I reached my own quiet fireside after the reiterated shouts and plaudits half dead, my joy, my thankfulness were of too solemn and over-powering a nature to admit of words or even tears. My Father, my Husband and myself sat down to a frugal, cold meat supper in a silence uninterrupted except by joyful exclamations from Mr Siddons. My Father enjoyed his refreshments but occasionally stop'd short and laying down his knife and fork, . . . let forth such abundant showers of delicious tears that they actually poured down into his plate. We soon parted for the night, and I, worn out with continual broken rest, anxiety, and laborious exertion after an hour's introspection, fell into a sweet and profound sleep.

So ended the day of "the first Tragic Actress now on the English stage", as recorded in the *Post*. What Sarah herself always spoke of as her "Trying Moment" was safely negotiated.

The remainder of her roles were fitted into the season's repertory. A venerable James Boaden, his steel-rimmed spectacles still tilted athwart his nose, was later to record that literally the greater part of the spectators were too ill to use their hands in applause—"Mrs Siddons," according to Tom Davies, writing a few years later, "absolutely depressed the spirits of her most admired public with her Euphrasia in *The Grecian Daughter* followed hard on by Belvidera in *Venice Preserved*, and *Jane Shore*," in which, according to the Venerable Boaden, she caused "sobs and shrieks and those tears, which Manhood at first struggled to suppress, but at length grew proud of indulging. Fainting fits, long and frequent, alarmed the House filled almost to suffocation."

Horace Walpole, however, was determined not to be, like the common herd, "bowled over by the Thespian Conqueror":

> Mr Crawford [he wrote to the Countess of Ossery] asked me if I did not think her the best actress I ever saw? I said "By no means; we old folk are apt to be prejudiced in favour of our first impressions." She is a good figure, handsome enough, though neither nose nor chin according to the Greek standard, beyond which both advance a good deal. Her hair is either red, or she has no objection to its being thought so ... her arms are not genteel.

We can leave Sarah, then, tasting her success while her public moans, moons, swoons, cries out and weeps, until an honour undreamed of in her barn-storming days descended on her— Royal Patronage.

"I am an enthusiast for her," announced His Majesty, to recourse again to the Diary of Miss Fanny Burney. "Quite an enthusiast. I think there was never any player in my time so excellent—not Garrick himself, I own it. What? What?"

But Kezia and Salubria would have taken heart had they

known that to some degree their opinion of the popular Show-Off was shared by the stylish Diarist: "I could not concur where I felt so differently," notes Miss Burney.

"I was much disappointed in my expectations," she confided to her Diary, on the first occasion Mrs Siddons was summoned to Buckingham House to read to the Queen:

I found the heroine of Tragedy sublime, elevated and solemn; in manner quiet and stiff; in voice, deep and dragging; and in conversation, formal, sententious, calm and dry . . . whether fame and success have spoiled her, or whether she only possesses the skill of representing and embellishing materials with which she is furnished by others, I know not; but still I remain disappointed.

Set a woman to judge a woman.

It was well-known that His Majesty hardly ever, on his visits to the Theatre, chose a Tragedy—rather the Monarch enjoyed a hearty laugh at a comedian, in which he did not differ greatly from some of the other monarchs who were to succeed him. Yet her Euphrasia, her Belvidera, her Calistra, her Jane Shore and her Isabella, were honoured by the presence of the King and Queen.

"She graciously commended herself by total repose in certain situations. This is," he said, "a quality in which Garrick failed. He never could stand still. He was a great fidget."

The town flocked to see la Siddons in this and la Siddons in that. Even Dr Johnson was drawn, much against his better judgment initially, to see the new idol of the Metropolis. "The last time I was at a play," he protested, "I was ordered there by Mrs Abingdon, or Mrs Somebody. I do not remember who." And Mrs Thrale, meeting Mrs Siddons at some society reception, exclaimed: "Why, this is a leaden goddess we are all worshipping."

In time, these two redoubtable ladies, Mrs Siddons and Mrs Thrale, were to become great friends.

Miss Burney and Mrs Thrale may well have diverged from public opinion in the matter of the graces of Sarah Siddons, but King George the Third knew better, and at the end of her triumphant season at Drury Lane appointed her, at Queen Charlotte's particular request, to the post of Reading Preceptress to the Princesses, "A post," as she was to remark drily to her biographer, "ALL HONOUR, but NO SALARY." There were, however, pickings. The Queen unclasped from her own neck "a magnificent gold chain with a cross of many-coloured jewels" and gave it to Sarah—who called it her "badge of honour"—and she always had the privilege of driving to and from Buckingham House in a Royal carriage. Yet her tastes remained simple enough: "Oh for a piece of Langford brown bread," she was heard to exclaim one day on being decanted from the Royal carriage: and be her homely suppers never more plain, her Sid remarked that she was "an excellent forker!"

Towards the end of this, her first season on her return to the Lane, so famous were the fits and swoons to which she reduced her audiences that the orange-women were said to cry nothing but "Hartsthorn" and "Lavender drops".

BOOK TWO
They could have danced all night

❖❙ Chapter 1 ❙❖

Two young ladies, Sally and Maria, newly returned from a Calais finishing school, sat stitching in the withdrawing room of Sarah Siddons' London house in Great Marlborough Street. Their almost unnatural pallor could just be discerned through the diffused October twilight. The flicker of candles not so much illuminated as punctuated the gathering close of day. The fire was almost out.

Maria, the younger, more spirited of the sisters shivered and drew her shawl closer around her throat. "Our sweet Mama is kept late at rehearsals, this afternoon; do you think I should put a poker to the fire, Sister?" She removed the sprig of holly Mrs Siddons insisted both her daughters should wear at the throat; thorny reminders to hold their heads high and Queenly.

"Maria!" Sally, the elder, more sensitive of the sisters, with the gentler nature and sweeter smile, sounded scandalised. "Maria! You cannot have forgotten how darling Mama enjoys to give the logs a well-placed kick and make the sparks fly."

"Mama never fails to make the sparks fly, particularly when she has had a bout with Papa," retorted Maria, pertly.

Time, then, has passed since Mrs Siddons made her return, trembling, to the Theatre Royal, Drury Lane. Some dozen years or more, to be as precise as History, viewed through the haze of fiction, will allow. A handful of time, then, but enough to confirm Mrs Siddons as a matron. Physically her rounded contours were advanced into *embonpoint*, which is to say the curves of pliant softness still adorn the darling of Bench and Side-Box, but have, by this time, taken on something of an air of being kept in place by a hidden armoury of Whalebone. Her mannerisms were less kittenish, more starkly etched.

Both professionally and personally she "filled her arch". But perhaps this was more startling off-stage than on. And then her nature and affections had hardened since those coaching days of hers from Bath to Bristol and, a human pendulum, from Bristol to Bath. Now her journeyings were punctuated by sittings for portraits since painters seemed to spring up like dog-roses in hedgerows at whatever town she alighted, pleading to paint her admired features and long nose; at least this is what Sir Joshua Reynolds, throwing down his brush, was to pronounce that organ: "Great Heavens, Woman! Is there no end to your nose!" The portrait-painters clamoured and Mrs Siddons, if she did not entirely melt and unbend to them, at least co-operated, endowing the canvas with as much as she could summon of her histrionic skills; just as in our own times Stars of the Stage, Models and Professional Personalities co-operate with the cameras in the impersonal cause of Professional Publicity. And then, was not the ardent young portraitist, Thomas Lawrence, in London? Impulsive, tempestuous and made much of by the Nobility whose homes this son of an ambitious Innkeeper penetrated to paint Milord and his good Lady, and the cream of the whirling world of fashion.

A sharp rapping at the front door. A heavy tread and the

sound of muttering in the hall, as Betsy Noakes, her bustling days for ever gone, answered the rapping. "Knock, knock, knock," muttered the old crone. "Shakespeare, drat the man!" she added inconsequently. A chill gust of the east wind. A pitter-patter of sandals on the bare tiles of the anteroom, and a mountain of flowers from tight little bundles of the humble, fragrant, violet, to elegant sprays and clusters of Georgian roses. "New-fangled fiddle-faddle," in the eyes of Nannie Noakes, when called on to bring in yet more of Sir Josiah Wedgwood's urns and vases. And behind and almost buried beneath them, both arms full, is la Siddons.

"Mama! Mama!"

"Mama! dear, sweet Mama!"

Sarah Siddons ignored her darling Daughters. She strode over to the smouldering fire and gave the logs a well-placed kick, articulating with her customary clarity: "Painters take that [kick] and that [kick]; it is well deserv'd—anapaestic substitution!" The Siddons girls exchanged a look. Like a cutting wind, their sweet Mama's temperament had veered due east—perilous quarter indeed.

And where was Mr Lawrence, both daughters silently asked themselves? They regarded each other with a shrewd surmise. Could he have displeased their sweet Mama? He could.

Mrs Siddons punched a pillow, tossed it on to the *chaise-longue* where it alighted on a bank of bouquets, breaking some of the choicest blooms, from which fragrant edifice it toppled over and on to the floor. She ignored it, sat bolt upright in a chair designed by Mr Sheraton for that purpose, and kicked off her sandals. She looked every inch as Queenly without them as a very vexed Queen could look! She surveyed her daughters and smiled grimly. Just so would Queen Lear have looked had the Bard thought fit to create her.

"How goes the fever, my little Maria? Caesura?" she finished inexplicably.

"Quite gone, almost," Maria responded hopefully.

Mrs Siddons beckoned—the gesture would have done nicely for the Ghost in Hamlet. She laid a snowy hand on her younger daughter's ivory brow. "No Assembly for you tonight, my Child," she pronounced. "I myself shall inform Miss Fanny Burney and drop the note in on my way to the banquet at Royal Lodge tonight."

Maria pouted and hung her head as a pale rose might whose bloom has grown too heavy on its stem. She was young and pretty, turbulent and silly and spoilt and infinitely touching; and ill of the Pallor. And she loved to dance. Both girls were passionately fond of dancing.

"My partner must be odious indeed if I am not pleased to dance," Sally declared while Maria bewailed the fact that even when she was not too poorly to attend a Ball—a rare occasion—she was unable and indeed forbidden to dance.

"Your holly, young Ladies." The young ladies, caught out, replaced their thorny persecution.

"And you, my Sally? How is your cough this eve?—anapaestic substitution," she pointed out, for she had fallen into the habit off-stage, as on, of speaking in blank verse.

"Less persistent, dear Mama, almost . . . almost . . ."

But even as she gallantly strove to deny it, her slender shoulders shook in an uncontrollable fit of coughing which she sought to strangle in her chest and throat.

"No dancing, Daughter, that is very clear," diagnosed her sweet Mama, and, still in her stockinged feet, made a swift exit left; so might Juliet have hastened to her love, to her Romeo.

"Mama!"

"Oh sweet Mama!" wailed her desolate Daughters, but the door had closed with something of a slam behind her.

It had not been so much Mr Sheridan's forward behaviour in the carriage—it was too cold for the calèche—which had disturbed Mrs Siddons' perilous calm, but that it was not the portraitist, young Lawrence, behaving in that shocking manner which she had every reason to expect.

"Mr Sheridan!" she had protested. "I trust you will comport yourself with all propriety." But the wily Sheridan had only pressed closer to her. "If you do not I shall immediately let down the glass and desire my footman to show you out."

Besides she had a shrewd but accurate idea that Richard Brinsley Sheridan thought it might be more difficult for her Sid to press for the return of the two thousand pounds owed to her—which had mysteriously got itself into Mr Sheridan's coffers—if there were a sentimental interlude with his wife. "My precious two thousand pounds, swallowed up in that drowning gulf, from which no plea of right or justice can save its victims!"

"Poor Mama, with no Mr Lawrence to keep her black mood at bay," said Sally, as always, sweetness itself.

"I fancy he has other fish to fry!"

"Maria, how can you be so heartless? And vulgar?"

The sisters settled down by the offended fire, for it was smouldering after Mrs Siddons' high-footed treatment, and each took up her needlework, and a pretty enough picture they made, Sarah with her *petit-point* chair-back of roses and lilacs— how bright the silks looked—and Maria, still pouting a little, with her *pointe d'hongroise* executed in coloured wools and— which was characteristic—more quickly achieved.

"Poor Mama, she looked quite furious."

"It is all that rehearsing. It leaves her with no time for any-thing."

"Or anyone?"

"Except young Mr Lawrence, of course."

"Of course."

"It is certain that she has little time for dear Papa."

"Poor dear Papa."

"He seems so elderly, poor dear Papa, beside her radiance."

"And Mama seems so radiantly young."

"Seems," said Maria, and had she not been a loving Daughter, one could have sworn there was malice in her emphasis. "I shall not be surprised if Mr Lawrence did not pay me a call this evening."

"Us," her elder sister corrected her, "pay *us* a call, Maria."

"Yes, yes, Sister, he will ask for *us*, but as you know his sighs will be addressed to me." *Impasse!*

"What idle nonsense has lodged itself in your pretty little pate, Child!"

Maria stamped her foot and dug her chin in the air much as her dear Mama, her dear Mama's Mama and her Sainted Great-Grandma had done before her in somewhat similar circumstances: "I am seventeen years of age, or soon will be—passed sixteen anyway!"

"As I said, a Child," her maddening sister had reasons of her own for not changing her tune.

"Think of Juliet," Maria Siddons urged.

"Young ladies ripen more quickly in a Southern climate," said her temperate elder sister.

"Why did I have to be born a Kemble?" wailed Maria. "If Mama had been an Italian actress I might have been a married young lady and a mother by this time."

Sally Siddons smiled her sweet, patient smile. It always maddened Maria the more. "But we do not live in Verona, sister, we live here in London."

"And in Bath."

"And adjacent to a dozen Theatre Royals in Winter Resorts. And you are my little Sister Maria, not Juliet. Merciful Heavens a' made a bad end! And when our eager, eloquent, tip-toe Mama plays her there is not a dry eye in whatever theatre it is."

"When Mrs Crawford shrieks and groans rows of spectators start from their seats."

"But our eloquent Mama goes further."

"Much," said the mutinous Maria.

"When Mama shrieks the whole house shrieks with her."

"I know," said Maria, forlornly.

"Believe me, little sister, if young Mr Lawrence sighs for anyone it will be for our lovely Mama."

"But she is turned of thirty."

"You forget, Sister, that our magical Mama can enchant every gentleman in the audience into believing she is whatever age she wishes to be. Why, so many fine and well-regarded portraitists have immortalised her, yet her potent magic defeats them and in despair they try again—even Mr Gainsborough and Mr Reynolds; and Mr Flaxman is modelling her head for Queen of the Chess Men. It is inevitable that when Mr Lawrence calls and condescends to chat with us it is only to while away the minutes until our beautiful Mama appears, a goddess in his eyes."

"Time will tell," said stubborn Maria, with a sagacity beyond her handful of years.

And even as she spoke the front door bell pealed and jangled. Just time to snatch the sprigs of holly from their throats. Just time to pat their hair. Both turned expectant faces to the sitting-room door.

But it was only that boring James Boaden, his steel spectacles more perilously posed on his long thin nose than ever, coming to call on Mama. It seemed that young Lochinvar had come out from the West and equally young Master Boaden had been engaged to show him the sights of London—or those deemed suitable for one so green and unused to travel.

The Siddons sisters sighed and settled to a long dull evening with their sweet Mama's ungainly admirer. Nannie Noakes, her lace-making cushion and pins in hand, installed on Mr Sheraton's least uncomfortable straight-backed settle, as chaperone: and to her it seemed that both her charges were mere children and that only the other day they were squealing, squalling and squabbling in their country cots.

There was a clanging and a pealing at the front-door bell.

"Drat it," said Nannie Noakes, and scuttled away to answer the insistent caller: Thomas Lawrence.

Maria ran forward, certain that the call was for her. But Lawrence was bending over Sally's hand; and Sally was smiling her sweet and assured smile.

·❧ Chapter 2 ❧·

ACTRESSES, the spirited creatures, in the 1780s were popped into any old productions of contemporary classics like the Ballerinas of time, the present. They were allotted marks by their public very much as show jumpers are today. Mrs Crawford, for instance, though once "most elegant in her deportment became soon both rough and coarse, and her appearance became that of an old man". Worse in Sarah Siddons' eyes was that the wretch had pre-empted a shriek and a groan "that brought rows of spectators to their feet with a jerk". Nothing for it, poor darling, but to shriek louder, and when Sarah Siddons shrieked her house shrieked with her, fortunately.

A charming list of theatrical left-overs placed at Mrs Siddons' disposal at the Lane makes a sufficient image. The underlinings are the clerk's:

A drop wood
A drop palace

A town flat

Three chambers, holes in one of them, the doors of the drop
  chamber very bad

Prison

Canal garden

Blasted Heath. *Macbeth*

Cut wood. *Hamlet*

Cave with catacomb painted on the back

Gothic palace

Long wood, a hole in it

Part of the hovel in *The Sorcerer*

Statue in *Merope*

Patty's house, very bad

Doctor's brick house in *Mercury Harlequin*

Rialto

The statue of Osiris

Aimsworth's house, one stile

Battlement, torn

Tomb in the *Grecian Daughter*

Library

An old Patagonian chamber in *Mother Shipton*

Water-fall in the *Dargle*, very bad

Altar piece in *Theodosius*

Palace arch of the Corinthian Order

Two large wood rings, greatly damaged

One piece of clouding, very old and little worth

Five pairs of Gothic wings (fire holes in the canvas)

Five small tents

Juliet's balcony

Balcony in *The Suspicious Husband*

The Bridge of *King Arthur*

Juliet's bed

Five sky borders

Four gentlemen's turbans

Six common ditto
Three white hats
Bow quiver and Bonnet for Douglas
A small map for Lear
One shepherd's hat
Four small paper tarts

Seven spears [for carrying?]
Nine rods, one crook
Two shapes
An old toy fiddler
One goblet .
Edgar's hat
One pediment for Banquet
Lantern for *Grecian Daughter*
One pair of scissors
Two pieces of scantling to hang clothes on
Four very small rocks
Eleven metal thunderbolts
67 wood ditto
Five stone ditto
Three baskets for thunderbolts
One canopy
The pedestal and horse in *The Sorcerer*, Out of repair
Hob's Well: two water wheels; boat in the *Dargle*
Four long barrels with multiplying wheels
Rack in *Venice Preserv'd*
Elephant in *The Enchanted Lady*. Very bad
Alexander's car, some of it wanting
The Star King Albert cut across

Left in the trunk in Mrs Barry's Room
[She had to dress handsomely to distract attention from a
lop-sided mouth. And Mrs Siddons was allowed to dip in.]

A black velvet dress and train
A yellow and silver dress
A Spanish blue and white thread satin ditto
A pink coloured silk ditto
A puckered white satin petticoat
A blue thread satin robe
Ten white linen dresses
Two stuffed petticoats and a jacket
A red puckered dress
A white dress covered with gauze
Four dresses in *Artaxerxes*
A pair of shepherd's breeches

—whereof the doting James Boaden, passing through on his way to lend a hand at Mrs Molesworth's Holiday House, stopped to sigh "For the Dear Woman's own Rosalind, no doubt."

And there were in addition, sundry cars, trophies and other mechanical transports for spectacles and triumphs; such as her famous passage across stage, when Mrs Siddons in the person of Volumnia in *Coriolanus*, in a garb of A pink coloured silk ditto, broke rank and with head erect and hands firmly pressed to her bosom, as though to suppress by manual force its triumphant swellings, towering above all around her, was borne almost tipsily across the Battlements (torn).

So much for verisimilitude.

·❦ Chapter 3 ❧·

FIRE, we have been told by a great many eighteenth-century commentators and historians worth their tinder-boxes, and a handful of writers from our own days, was a constant peril in the playhouses of Sarah Siddons' time, which must have been much in the minds of playgoers hemmed in, as they were, like sardines in a tin, in an age when theatres were lit by unbated candles, lamps and flambeaux. To set the scene on fire it took only the carelessness of some gin-fuddled stagehand, and whatever may have been lacking in Mr Sheridan's majestic Theatre Royal, Drury Lane, rebuilt and refurbished only four years since by the Brothers Adam, staggering stagehands at least were not in short supply.

When first the doors had been flung open to the admiring public it had fallen to the lot of the eager James Boaden, who had chanced to have some midnight oil to burn, to compose a Prologue—and how better to burn midnight oil than in covering a page in somewhat insistent rhyme, even if he did only get the

commission because he would gladly have composed it without
a fee, ever a strong argument with Sheridan.

The prologue was to be spoken by Miss Young (in private
life, Mrs Pope—no relation) and it included the, in the light
of hindsight, trouble-shooting lines:

> The very ravages of fire we scout,
> For we have wherewithal to put them out,
> In ample reservoirs, our firm reliance,
> Whose streams set conflagration at defiance.

Famous last words, if ever the Fates had heard them.

On the night when staggering stagehands and leaping flames
came to the eighteenth-century crunch, Mr Sheridan was in
the House of Commons. Hansard duly reported that "A cry of
Fire! Fire! frequently interrupted the latter part of the Right
Hon. Secretary's speech, and Mr Sheridan in a loud voice
stated across the table that the Drury Lane Theatre was on fire.
Lord Temple thought the House should adjourn—a compassionate suggestion. But Sheridan said 'with much calmness'
that whatever might be the extent of the calamity he did not
consider it of a nature worthy to interrupt their proceedings
on so great a national question." The fire raged with such a fury
that it illumined Lincoln's Inn Fields. Fortunately it was Lent
and there was no audience to stampede.

But James Boaden was on the spot, having abandoned the
Mail Coach to the Highlands bound, so highly commended by
Mr Boswell, at an early stage of the old rock-and-shake bones.
He had reached the burning building just as the great statue of
Apollo, which honoured the topmost part of the façade, sank into
the rising sea of flames. Two days later he dipped his quill into
its well of Indian ink and wrote:

In less than one quarter of an hour the fire spreading one

unbroken flame over the whole of the immense pile, from Brydges Street to Drury Lane, and the rapidity of the flames was such that before midnight the whole of the interior was one blaze.

The appearance was tremendously *grand*. Never did I behold so immense a body of flame; and the occasional explosions that took place were awful beyond description.

When Sheridan finally left the House he strolled to Drury Lane to sit in the Piazza Coffee Shop, watching his noble Theatre burn to ashes.

Someone marvelled at his composure, but he replied with a revival of his sometime classic wit: "A man may surely take a glass of wine by his own fireside."

Sarah Siddons in a letter to Lady Harcourt joins the general wailing:

. . . Not a fragment of the whole structure was discoverable at six, at which time my brother first heard of it, and he declared that at that time it was so completely destroyed that you could not have known a building had stood there. The losses of scenes, dresses, etc., are, as you may imagine, incalculable and irreparable. I have lost everything, all my jewels and lace, which I have been collecting for thirty years, and which I could not purchase again, for they were all really fine and curious. I had a point veil which had been a toilette of the poor Queen of France, near five yards long, and which could not have been bought for anything like so little as a thousand pounds, destroyed, with dresses of my own of great value for costumes. In short, everything I had in the world of stage ornament is gone, and literally not one vestige left of all that has cost me so much time and money to collect. We are to act at the Opera, and next Monday I shall attempt the character of Lady Randolph there. My poor dear brother has to begin the world again. It is a glorious feeling to see how many noble and friendly attentions have been shown to him on this occasion.

Lord Guildford and Lord Mountjoy have offered to advance any sum of money they can raise by any means. My head is confused, I scarce know what I write, but you, my dear Lady H, will have the goodness to excuse any incoherence in these circumstances.

The Prince too, has been so good and gracious. Everybody is good and kind, and, please God, we shall still do well. Adieu.

John Philip Kemble, no longer merry, indeed, downright gloomy and married to the Theatre Royal prompter's daughter ("What Kemble ever needed a prompt?" muttered a heavy black cloud above Bow Street, loyal but inaccurate, as it collided with a tumulus which previous to impact had been nowhere to be seen, resulting inexplicably in instant thunder and lightning totally local to the corner of Bow Street and Floral Street), joined forces with his towering sister, and, having suffered for some years the bitter discrepancy between Sheridan's personal charm and his unfathomable financial duplicity, installed himself and his sister sumptuously enough in the Bow Street Theatre Royal, an orange-throw from the busily rebuilding Mr Sheridan in the poor razed Drury Lane Theatre, where John Philip had given his vacillating Prince, on September 24th, 1803, and where his doe-eyed sister had given her Isabella three days later.

As to the Bow Street Theatre, the auditorium changed several times during the magnificent span of Sarah Siddons' ascendancy. The galleries were decorated anew in blue and silver "with elegant columns" to replace the former crimson and gold colour scheme: which was warm and theatrical, but, in a sense, vulgar.

"The front of the boxes," chronicled the still young but already balding Boaden, who had abandoned Lord Ullin's daughter, whose son he had been tutoring in Latin, with ne'er a backward glance. He had taken the bed-and-breakfast on the fourth floor back in a rooming house in St Giles'—not a salubrious neighbourhood, but an equidistant prompter's hiss from the Phoenix-like rising Theatre Royal, Drury Lane, and the Bow Street Theatre—while civilising the country lad Jim Hawkins, who ever since his escapade on Treasure Island had inexplicably taken to brandishing a leathern bottle in the small hours of the night, bellowing, "Yo, ho! ho! and a bottle of rum." But to return to the refurbishing of the temple of John Philip's art:

> The front of the boxes was uniformly painted with a beautiful dead white and gold, without aid of gaudy colour or tinsel decoration . . . the side continuation of the two shilling gallery was converted into boxes called 'the slips'. A drop-curtain in oil and water-colours, representing the Royal Arms supported by cherubs formed a very superb picture; the exact copy of that in the Theatre in Lincoln's Inn Field in the time of Cibber [pronounce him as you will], Wilks and Booth. The ceiling was ornamented in an artistic manner without any of the old-time heaviness.

Here, Boaden, his steel-rimmed glasses tilted more acutely than ever, laid aside his quill and pondered the majesty of London's theatres.

Outside Drury Lane, London, as the Siddons and the Kembles knew it, would have been a city of green and pleasant squares, gardens and walks. The fields opposite Sloane Square basked peacefully under its elms, the houses aired their calm façades and pillared porticoes.

This then, was the London through which Sarah Siddons was

carried in a chaise, or bowled by in a caleche with her daughters, or with her constant swain, Thomas Lawrence, without her daughters.

Time passed, reckoned by Mrs Siddons in terms of seasons in London, seasons in Bath, Bristol, Cheltenham, Brecon, the good-Lord-knows-where-not, York, and back to London again. Or, in the roles she played such as Three Isabellas, two Countess Orsinis, five Euphrasias, plain Jane—number and source unspecified. Complacent, she would tick time off on her mittened fingers as she was carried through the calm London places and squares on her way to sit to Sir Joshua in Leicester Square, or to Mr Gainsborough in That Hat, in his magnificent mansion, Schomberg House, in Pall Mall, looking more like the Duchess of Devonshire than Her Grace could ever look.

And it was in shady Soho Square, while her absent Mama was being bowled along to sit for Mr Romney, that delightful Sally Siddons became clandestinely affianced to her Mama's beau, Thomas Lawrence. He had stolen out from his rooms in nearby Greek Street to keep this tryst, hopefully to avoid a Siddons family brou-ha-ha! to which his beloved's famous Mama and her devoted younger sister, not to mention Nannie Noakes, would most audibly have given voice, and narrowly avoiding a fringe of Bailiffs or lurking creditors.

We, at this distance from all those Mrs Hallers, Elviras, Hermiones, or Ariadnes in *The Rival Sisters*, or to put the point more objectively, at this distance in time, we of the Welfare State civilised, can ignore the narrow unwholesomeness of lanes winding off Fleet Street; the mud on the unswept side-walks in winter and early spring; the garbage rotting in the gutters; fogs, harbingers of shouting link-boys and reeling, drunken chairmen; the dark low-ceilinged shops where the apprentices slept under counters; the forlorn bundles of rags that were sleeping children, worn out from the heavy labours of the day, as we stroll in our imagination with Sally and Tom in the eternal sunshine of their elegant age; or as they paused to gaze at each other, a pair of lovers in a painting by the master of masters, as though time had held its breath and their love would last for ever.

But death from open drains or other foul exhalations was not, as one of her many biographers points out, the only danger to the Family Siddons' way of life. There were also the footpads who lurked on the way out to the Grove of Westbourne, where Mrs Siddons was some day to dwell and often visited, and on her visits to the Queen at her country residence on that wild heath, Richmond Park, or at Kew.

. . . One moonlit night in lilac time a highwayman came riding, riding, riding, over the heath that lay nearby Kew, towards which Mrs Siddons, in a hired barouche, chanced to be driving, driving, driving. The highwayman and the actress were pursuing a headlong course, riding, riding, riding and driving, driving, driving right past the old inn door. The highwayman — he was a very green and inexperienced highwayman — swerved dangerously and by good fortune missed the carriage — just. He reined in his horse in a fine old clatter — no time for a neigh. Wildly he waved an ancient blunderbuss at an extremely ruffled Mrs Siddons, who realised in a flash that the creature was not answering to his cue. Never slow to prompt the forgetful, she rose to the occasion:

"Halt, who goes there?" Her voice was a clarion call to courage.

"M . . m . . me," mumbled the inexperienced highwayman.

They seemed to have got their lines mixed. "And who may you be?" Mrs Siddons' voice was at its crispest. No green gunman was going to catch her shivering in her corset.

"M . . Mister Halfred Noyes never gave me no name. Reckon I'm a bastard."

The silence was absolute. Sarah Siddons, never at a loss for an iamb with anapaestic substitution, broke it: "Reckon you're right, my man, but let us proceed. Your money or your life?"

The highwayman, green as a china orange (also unripe), snivelled. He felt in his poacher's pouch for a rag with which to wipe away his tears, and in groping for it he dropped his blunderbuss.

"That's better," said Mrs Siddons, and with all the Majesty she could command (and could that lady command Majesty!) she dismounted. "Out Mr Boaden," she commanded the other passenger, "follow me." She waved her umbrella. "Be nothing daunted."

"Oh dear," said the something daunted James Boaden. It was indeed a pretty kettle of fish for a future biographer to be in, and him without a quill and ink. The moon sailed out from behind a particularly threatening cloud as he stumbled, admiring but shortsighted.

The highwayman's horse, young Dobbin, let out a neigh and pawed the ground. It was time someone paid a little attention to him, he considered. But the stern lady with the plumes in her bonnet—were they eatable?—held out no sugar. She was too busy retrieving the highwayman's blunderbuss with as much dignity as she could summon. She pointed it at its owner. "You up there," she said, "are you a married highwayman?"

"Oh aye!" The would-be robber perked up visibly. He was, he would like it to be understood, quite an experienced and regular husband. It was only hard times that had driven him to this desperate pass.

"And has your—um—union been blessed by Church?" asked Boaden, interested.

"Vicar of Bray, Sir, no less!" boasted the highwayman.

"Any babes?" asked Mrs Siddons. Before everything she was a Mother, she told herself—frequently.

"One little girl and another on the way. And my Susan's a' bed and that is why . . . is why . . ."

Sarah Siddons finished the sentence for him. "And that is why you are holding us to ransom, my good man. And they are like to starve if you do not give a more convincing, more terrifying performance!"

The highwayman hung his head.

"Well, come with me and I will rehearse you," said Sarah Siddons. "Mr Boaden, light the flambeau and bring it to yonder greensward. And you, coachman, stop cowering and light the other."

And there in the leaping light of the torches, Sarah Siddons took the hesitant highwayman through his lines until he was word-perfect, and even strutting a little, to the approval of a single watchful cloud. It would have done exactly the same itself, it averred, and proffered a certain star a swig of nectar—or was it gin? It was not for nothing that its grand-daughter, Mrs Siddons, had been née Kemble.

Back from her torch-lit interval, Sarah Siddons resumed the drama of her life. The family drawing-room bore something of the appearance of a battlefield whence all living souls had fled; all, that is, save a desperate Thomas Lawrence, the villain who had just declared his love for her elder daughter Sally.

On the seat by the fireside, his intended sister-in-law, Maria Siddons, had swooned dead away, her ivory countenance pale as her wasting life. On the rocking-chair, her lace-making cushion with its array of pins for patterning still lying in her lap, Sally, the twenty-one-year-old darling of his heart this season, had swooned with equal vigour. Supine on the *chaise-longue* England's First Lady of the Stage, his future mother-in-law, lay deprived of her senses while on the sofa beneath the window Nannie Noakes had contrived to faint with one stout righteous leg in the air, a feat known only to herself, and it was all his fault for daring to aspire to the hand of his sweet Sallie. Which lady should he assist back to life first? Her mother? He shrank from the great tragedienne's *dies irae*. That spoilt little brat, her wilful, ever-ailing sister? His sweet long-suffering Sally? But even as he took a step towards his beloved he paused. Betsy Noakes first. She had an uncommon—and in this house much exercised—gift for dealing with fainted ladies, wielding snuff, burning feathers and slapping cheeks with joyous abandon. Indeed, no sooner was the Siddons' drawing-room resounding to the fluttering sighs and dove-like moans of the ladies coming back to life, than the great Sarah Siddons sat bolt upright.

"Where was I?" She took in the unhappy Mr Lawrence, the very picture of woe. "Oh yes! Wait till I recount the circumstances to dear Sally's Papa! He'll set about you with his riding whip, I should hope. How could you do this damnation thing to me? And Sally a chit of a child with a weak constitution!"

Meanwhile the high-metalled Maria, finding she was not after all, in Heaven, turned on her affectionate sister: "How could you do this thing to me?" and she coughed something alarming.

Sally, brought so rudely back to the present, heaved a sigh and turned to her beloved: "How could we behave so monstrously to our sister? I am ashamed of our heartlessness, ashamed, Sir!"

And now Nannie Noakes voiced her thoughts: "How could you behave so shamelessly to US," she demanded? "All of us," she amended.

Small wonder young Mr Lawrence fled the battlefield.

A year, like a wounded snake, dragged its long length along. (Not Shakespeare.) A year punctuated with the hopes, fears and tears of the ladies Siddons, each after her own manner, and not forgetting—who could?—the forthright scoldings of Nannie Noakes. "Fashionable painter is it? Cornstooks and cabbages! He did not do a mort of good for my features. Though I grant you he painted the Devil on *our* door, bad cess to him!" Here stout-hearted Betsy had recourse to the gin bottle she carried around in her apron pocket, labelled "Strong Waters if Needed", which, in her advancing years, how frequently it was, while the shade of Sarah Siddons' imperishable Mama's Mama looked approvingly down on her.

It was indeed a fever-filled world for the emotional sisters Siddons, both young ladies in love with the same suitor, both with such tender, vulnerable hearts, both failing in health and visibly fading from their bright world. And what a torn world it was for their famous, their adored Mama, with a desperate and, she thought, hidden love for her elder daughter's professed though not officially acknowledged beau; a love perhaps hidden even from herself. Poor fond Sarah Siddons, who by now had to make do with the cold porridge which was all that was left from the ardent flame between herself and her Sid. ("Poor pretty Siddons", Mrs Piozzi, formerly Mrs Thrale, had noted, "a warm heart and a cold husband! But she'll come thro'.") Poor pretty Siddons indeed, hag-ridden by jealousy of the other woman, who, as ill-luck would have it, was also her darling Daughter, so appealing in her pallor, so radiant, and so much younger. It was as though the glow of her love for that talented spendthrift wretch, Lawrence, shone through her whole being, turning blood and bone to alabaster.

And if jealousy kept Mrs Siddons awake at nights, it was Finance that hounded her down the days. For was she not the only breadwinner of the family of invalids hers had become, and if an alliance between young Lawrence and a daughter were officially recognised and marriage followed, the Heavens forbid, was it not she herself who would be held responsible for a reckless son-in-law's debts? And was not the dear unfaithful boy threatened with bankruptcy by every mail-coach on the posting pendulum?

It was in this frame of mind that Mrs Siddons set forth on yet another bumpy circuit. Small wonder that she burst into tears in Leeds where she was giving her Juliet, when the usual rotund figure up in the gallery, a town crier by profession, enlivened her potion scene just as she was nerving herself to swallow the dread draught, with a good round bawl in his brassiest voice of "Soop it oop, lass!"

As for the rival sisters who were left so much to their own devices and ploys while their troubled Mama was being bumped about from Theatre Royal to Theatre Royal on her far-flung out-of-season Circuits—and flung was the right word for the bruised and coach-sick travellers in the Mail Coaches on the rough and rutted linking roads, in the iron-wheeled transport of her times—devices and ploys in which young Lawrence played a lion's share, to the outspoken rage of Nannie Noakes, driven by them to lacing her frequent mis-quotations from the Bard with Strong Waters if Needed. They were. ("Strong Water cannot quench love. Shashk's-hic-shpeare".)

Although Maria, wilful, sly, passionate, pretty and grasping and by now in her eighteenth year—"practically an old spinster" as she was wont to bemoan—was the further advanced of the two in her decline, as her sister, watching over her, said with a dismay bordering upon anguish, it was, in the event, poor, patient, sweet and unselfish Sally who fell ill of a consuming asthma that held her gasping to her room and which Nannie Noakes' steaming pans could not alleviate. Maria, the witch, seized her chance and contrived, in her sister's absence from society, to loosen the bond between Sally and the all too easily severed Lawrence; bonds that even the imperious Sarah Siddons had been unable to sever.

". . . Came home so late that I went to my room directly, and would not ring for candles that they might fancy I had been in *a great while*", reports the invalid. "*I felt* how to undress myself and came down about the middle of dinner. Asked where I had been, I told a *story* . . ."

And so, once again, Soho Square was the scene of a romantic trysting. Once again two lovers strolled there in a stolen trance like lovers in a painting by Mr Gainsborough, or paused to gaze into each others' eyes as though time stood still and their love would last forever. But this time they were Maria and the tempestuous Lawrence.

Fanny Kemble, Sarah Siddons' niece, has noted down for us that Master Tom, without Maria's constant presence, became

> deeply dejected, moody, restless and evidently extremely wretched. Violent scenes of the most painful emotion took place between himself and Mrs Siddons, to whom he finally, in a paroxysm of self-abandoned misery, confessed that he had mistaken his feelings for Sally and ended by imploring permission to transfer his affections from one to the other sister.

Confronted with Lawrence's switch of sisters, Mrs Siddons descended on her household in Great Marlborough Street to forbid everything all round, and a three-part dirge began. Maria, shrill and violent, took the treble clef, making great play with the hysterical *tessitura*. Sally, temperamentally a mezzo-soprano, had her customary serenity disturbed by the heartlessness of her supposed swain. And Sarah Siddons, contralto, livid with both daughters.

"But I love him—I love him!" shrilled Maria, a hectic flush suffusing her pretty, reproachful face.

"He loved me! Loved *me*!" mourned Sally as pink as was her sister and in an equal state of agitation.

"He is despicable," boomed their highly irritated Mama, "despicable!"

"Hic!" interpolated Nannie Noakes, turning the dirge into a Ribald Quartette.

". . . he loves *me*. He is *mine*." Maria sought to clinch it.

"He has been snatched from me, snatched!" Sally's mourning had some justification.

"Fiddlesticks," snapped their Mama.

"Hic," agreed Nannie Noakes again.

Their enraged Mama sought for the right word . . .

"Neither of you will marry that miscreant," she found.

"Mishcreant," echoed Nannie Noakes.

"Your Pa will never allow it."

"Pa!" said Nannie Noakes. She sniffed.

But just as the Family Siddons' dirge seemed to have arrived at the full close to its cadence, Mrs Siddons went smartly into a solo cadenza:

"Mine is the habitation of sickness and sorrow . . . my Poor Husband is Lame, Absolutely Walking on Crutches. Something the matter with his Knee, but whether from the Rheumatism or Gout or what it is, Heaven Knows; and the Terrible Dread of becoming A Cripple makes him Very Melancholy — alas! alas!"

Almost one can hear her Sid (bass) joining the coda antiphonally with a great many more alases!

And somewhere far, far away from Love's battlefield the painter Lawrence smiled in his dream of fair women.

·⊰ Chapter 4 ⊱·

AFTER that first burst of grief, Sally, as was her way, suffered in silence. Not so Maria. On the contrary, her plaints were loud, continuous and more and more hectic, more and more shrill, more and more insistent. The family doctor, called in to administer some soothing draught, warned her tight-lipped Mama that if she did not get her way in all things, and most certainly in matters of the affections, she would fret herself into a green sickness and thence, most dreaded ailment of the eighteenth century, into a Consumption.

"One woe doth tread upon another's heels," intoned Betsy Noakes. "The Bard," she added as an afterthought, "Scene . . ."

Lady Macbeth looked daggers at her. The Bard, Betsy Noakes was given to understand, was, or should be, her own exclusive material. And anyway, was she not the most Queenly Lady in the Lane—Lane? Nay, Land?

Betsy, completely quashed, drew comfort from her Apron Pocket. In spite of her woes Sally very nearly smiled.

Then Lady Macbeth remembered, as usual, that before everything she was a Mother. Nothing for it but to enter into a conspiracy of *laisser-faire* with her sweet Sally, to which end she drew aside for a Mother/Daughter/Nannie confabulation.

"I know, Daughter—none better—what it costs to see a former lover's happiness with," she drew a sharp breath, "Another."

Nannie Noakes nodded sagely. "Caesura," she said. Almost she might have been Sarah Siddons herself. Sally bent her head lower over the Eglantine she was embroidering on her tambour, that the telltale tears welling up in her eyes might be less easily discerned.

"Yet this is what it is my Duty to command you to do, my little Sally." No Queen could have held her head more regally. No Mother could have spoken more movingly.

Nannie Noakes applied her apron end to her eyes and her bottle of Strong Waters to her lips: here was need indeed. "Think of Shakespeare," she advised as she tilted the bottle.

"Libertine though he is, your younger sister has set her heart on him and must not be crossed, nay, not in her slightest whim. Has not Doctor Rumbelow spoken? Then grieve no more, sad fountains; Daughter, grieve no more! Though Heaven knows to break one's heart over an inconstant lover is the most natural thing in the world," said Sarah Siddons, recalled to a grief of her own.

"Promises are pie-crusts, meant to be broken," contributed Betsy Noakes, which did little to comfort either jilted one.

"Swear now upon this sword—" rang out the voice of the great Sarah Siddons—"your coral necklace will serve well enough, Child," she added *sotto voce*.

"I promise I will do my best," sobbed poor truthful Sally.

And from the spheres above a voice intoned: "Promishes, Promishes!"

As for that passionate little witch, Maria, even at this moment is she not penning a letter to her close friend, Miss Bird: "Nothing can be so delightful as the unremitting attention of those we love."

The outcome of so much whirling emotion was that an unwilling consent was wrung from Sarah Siddons to Maria's match, and her even slower agreement to pay off, as her daughter's dot, all her son-in-law presumptive's debts—earlier had not the wretch begged an adamant Sid to save him from the Bailiffs and bankruptcy by a long-term "loan", cash down? And Sally? Well, she soon resigned herself to watch the couple's happiness, a shared happiness which she must banish for ever from her own life.

Four weeks took wing, filled by the lovers with billing and cooing and embraces as passionate as the ever-watchful Nannie Noakes would allow.

> "They shall not, varmints, e'er be left alone
> Till holy Church incorporate two in one!"

"The Bard," Mrs Siddons got in while the none-too-pleased Betsy Noakes was drawing breath. "More or less," the great actress added.

And now Maria fell ill and was ordered to keep to her room. But we should not blame Doctor Rumbelow for the emotional turmoil this started all over again. How could a respected family doctor, who had long put love-sickness behind him, gauge the effect of the four weeks' separation of a spoilt young Adonis from his enchantress? How weigh the amorous balance of a vacillating bachelor?

Be that as it may, yet another, an utter confusion shook 40 Great Marlborough Street to its much-tried foundations. Just four weeks, yet they proved sufficient to bring the pendulum lover to his senses, satiety having set in.

Passionately as he had sought to marry Maria, it seemed that he now wanted out. What to do? Lawrence was not at a loss. He flung himself on the surprised shoulder of Mrs Siddons, his first love, gestured extravagantly, wept copiously, and begged to be returned to Sally who once more he idolised, or so he swore. Mrs Siddons promptly boxed his ears and, very sensibly, forbade him to see, write to, or linger in the vicinity of either daughter. "Stay away from our door," she intoned.

Sally gives us a glimpse of the state of play in a letter to Miss Bird: "A great, great change has taken place in our house," in which she wrote a deal less than the astounding truth. "When you write to our precious Maria, do not mention Mr Lawrence's name. *All that is at an end! . . .*"

Maria, too, took up her quill and addressed herself to Miss Bird:

I yet think I shall not live a long while. This is perhaps merely nerveous [spelling was never the strongest point of the Family Siddons] but I see nothing very shocking in the idea . . . I know you will be sorry to hear how ill I have been and how nerveous I still continue, tho' I am again mending.

The months passed and, we can well believe, were not without many anguished gaspings as Sally fought to breathe in and, even more painful, to breathe out; as Maria swooned and waxed feverish and her pallor, were it possible, increased, and Sid limped coughing in Bath. Filled, too, with a Mother's bumped-about anxieties as Mrs Siddons bounced from pillar to post—the pillars supporting the façades of Theatre Royals, the posts marking the entrance to whatever inn she was due to rest her head (for as Mrs Piozzi wrote, "I can no more imagine where Mrs Siddons actually is, than where Buonaparte is!")—to rest her head but not thereby to sleep, for fears in her foreboding heart for her two daughters and her husband and its achings no less for impulsive and inconstant Thomas Lawrence. The cost, too, of maintaining three invalids and keeping up her Public Face, her Art, and her colleagues' on Circuit lack of it, all these things told on her spirits and her health. Poor Sarah cursed the Provinces, so loyal to her and so vociferous in their appreciation, which drew her from the bed-side of her wasting Maria.

Charming Siddons [wrote Mrs Piozzi] is somewhere in the North, setting up the individuals of her family like ninepins for Fortune to bowl at and knock down again. She meantimes secures glorious immortality in both worlds.

It was with a heavy heart that, accompanied by Sally, her one solace, where she could keep an eye on her, she confided the care of Maria to Mrs Penelope Pennington in Clifton, by Bristol, who had successfully nursed her own daughter through the green sickness in years gone by, in the hope that those bracing Downs would exert their age-old magic on ailing lungs.

One midnight was to find the great actress, as often now it was to do, sitting at the small, upright Sheraton desk she always travelled with — such a useful prop — her quill in hand. "Dear Soul," she wrote to Mrs Pennington:

Dear Soul,
Add still to the numbers of your favours by telling me in every particular about my little Maria — her pulse, her perspirations, her cough, her *everything*.

And stricken Mother but true Thespian that she was she could not resist boasting, "I am playing every night *to very full houses!*" And then, for it was often said of her that she was "a good forker":

The Fat Cakes are quite as good as formerly—I verily believe I could have eaten half-a-dozen!

In August we find Sarah Siddons, upright as the desk she wrote at, eking out the closing afternoon's light.

I received your kind letter by the sick-bed of my poor Sally who has been somewhat ill here, and never out of her bed — except to have it made — since our arrival on Monday.

Here Mrs Siddons considered her quill. The sound punishing she had given those pillows had done much to relieve her pent-up tensions, temporarily. Then she heaved a cavernous sigh.

I do not flatter myself that my sweet Maria will be long continued to us. *The Will of God be done* but I hope she will not *suffer much*!

How vainly did I hope that sweet Sally had acquired the strength to throw off this cruel disorder! Instead it returns with increased velocity and violence. What a sad prospect this is for a future marriage! [Every woman is at heart a marriage broker?]

Could a husband's tenderness compensate for the separation from a Mother's? Would he not think it vastly inconvenient to have his comforts, his pleasures, his business interfered with? My friend the all-wise Doctor Johnson says that a man must be a *prodigy of virtue* who is not soon tir'd of an ailing wife and to say the truth a sick wife *must* be a *great misfortune*.

Adieu! Adieu! [Did the letter echo her mighty sigh?] I must go dress for Mrs Beverly [black bombazine]. My soul is well-tuned for scenes of woe and it is *a great relief* from the struggles to wear a face of cheerfulness at home, that I can, upon the *stage*, pour it all out on my innocent auditors . . .

The weeks trudged by. Sally grew better.
"Your letter," wrote Sarah Siddons to Mrs Pennington:

Your letter was given me this morning with another from my precious Maria, and this day have determined to deprive myself of the companionship of my darling Sally, who sets out in a post-chaise with a good soul, bound for Bristol, who has undertaken to be her Guardian . . . By this means she will avoid the distress of meeting with Mr L., who is come here on a visit.

I am harassed, fatigued to death and have all my things to prepare for tonight.

. . . The post-chaise, with many a rattle and clatter, had been pulled to a halt close enough to four in the morning. The Coachman blew his nose with a right royal blast, and peered through the mists of first light at the passengers about to board. It was a nipping and eager air. An elderly party, well wrapped up against it, clambered, making many attempts, into the coach and, swaying and puffing, slowly took his seat beside his Charge, an ivory-pale, invalidish lady, whose Ma, in clarion tones, was issuing last-minute instructions through the plate glass. Where had he seen that face before? The Coachman rubbed his chin. The Elderly Party's son, having got his breath back from his exertions in heaving his Pa on to the vehicle, was preparing to be gone. He adopted an attitude.

"Dear Papa," he enunciated, "Fare . . ." he paused for dramatic effect, "well," he concluded.

"Must be young Macready," the Driver, a gallery-goer, told himself. He had heard tell of them pauses . . .

Another Theatre Royal. Another Inn. The same upright desk and the same upright figure sitting at it:

Dear Soul,
I know not if Sally has told you that Mr L. was in Birmingham when she left me.

He has left this place without telling a soul whither he has gone . . .

wrote Sarah Siddons who clearly had her own idea of where he had gone in so much haste. Poor, troubled soul, she has no immediate need to worry—Maria is at this moment making Sally promise never to marry Lawrence.

> . . . I suppose he is almost mad with remorse, and think it likely that he may be at this moment in Clifton. I pray God his phrenzy may not impel him to some *Desparate Action*. But it is fit they should both be on their guard.

Mrs Siddons' fears of Lawrence's destination were only too well grounded. He made post-haste to Clifton, put up at an inn under an assumed name and sought out Mrs Pennington. Maria's feelings for him, he convinced himself, were but a sick-room fancy. He was not in the mood to allow them to bar his way to bliss, as he at this time saw it, with Sally.

To this end he dashed off a letter to disarm the sisters' temporary guardian dragon (Nannie Noakes having been left at Great Marlborough Street to take charge of Baby Cecilia, for Mrs Siddons had given birth again, somewhere along the line).

> . . . My name is Lawrence and I assure you that I stand in the most afflicting situation possible. I love—Miss Sally Siddons, and am decisively rejected by her. If I have touched her heart her present conduct is the more noble, correct and pure as every thought and action of her sweet character! "Yet Love will hope when Reason would Despair".
>
> Something I must do, and what better than to repose a confidence in a Woman of Sense and Honour, trust implicitly in her Candour, nor believe that I shall suffer by it . . .
>
> I have done it and perhaps *all of my future happiness is at stake, and in your power.*

I shall hope for your speedy answer. Only do not tell me that Passion should have its bounds and Love its caution . . . pray, if you can, pray give it tonight.

This letter had the effect the writer expected, or most of it. Mrs Pennington would see him, but "Not at my house".

It proved to be a trying interview. After listening to his threats — backed up with frenzied gestures — to kill himself if he could not see Sally, Mrs Pennington's quiet response that she "had seen such scenes better acted before", did little to soothe him: and further, that if he wished to secure her good offices a *rational* behaviour would be the best way to attain it. She promised to report daily on the state of the invalid and of any encouraging news which might raise his hopes of — eventually — Sally.

Whether in so doing she was playing Mrs Siddons false, or wanted to run with the hare and hunt the hounds, or just wished to put an end to an embarrassing interview, or, quite simply could not find it in her heart to resist his poutings and pleadings, the present writer could not say.

By return a note arrived at Mrs Pennington's establishment for the Lady of the house:

My blessings on you a thousand times . . . How strange it is to say that I am comparatively happy. What can have made me so . . . Dearest, dearest friend adieu! I will be compos'd, you shall see I can!

From now on almost one could be sorry for Lawrence, posting as he did between an injured mother and two wounded doves, with an understudy dragon relating all to each of them.

Here now is Mrs Siddons, her hartshorn never out of reach these days, penning yet another communication to Mrs Pennington:

Oh, my dear friend, how my heart bleeds for all the trouble and anxiety you have on my account. I shudder to think of the effect this wretched madman's phrenzy has had on you. If his own words are to be believed, I have more than once "shut upon him the gate of SELF-DESTRUCTION" by compromising as you now have done. Dear Sally is indeed an Angel . . . Think of the Tremendous Situation I was placed in! [Which was surely big enough to fill the proscenium of the nearest Theatre Royal, nay, of awe-inspiring Drury Lane itself.]

You now *know* the whole, and she has *seen* and *known* enough of *him* to make her *wary.*

You will warn this best loved of her Mother's heart—you, to whom it has been given to calm the sea when it roars wildest, for to that dreadful image have you well compared this unhappy man, on whom an EVIL FATE seems to attend, and wreaks its vengeance on all the most UNFORTUNATE SOULS WITH WHOM HE IS CONCERN'D.

A duteous Son, a tender Brother, a kind and zealous Friend: all these he is, and I bless God that you have reason'd him out of some extravagances that might have been dreadful in its present or future effects upon my POOR GIRLS, or on himself.

Good letters are like pearls as, to skip a century or so, Lytton Strachey reminds us: they are admirable in themselves but their value is infinitely enhanced when there is a string of them.

Scarcely had Mrs Siddons sealed the last, indeed the wax was still warm and sticky—when she could not forbear but to open the package again.

FRYDAY

. . . Do not let your affection for *me* induce you to be too resentful of this poor wretch's conduct. He has completely thrown away his *own happiness.*

[154]

Here Mrs Siddons doubtless looked up and into a hanging glass in which she could see reflected her own, at this moment, somewhat haggard beauty and sighed. She resumed writing:

Let us temper our indignation with pity.

We must also take into account that my agitated nerves acted, perhaps, more powerfully on me than there was just cause for. You tell me that you are to be "very good friends". Let us keep him quiet by all means that are *consistent* with our own safety. Do not leave it to him for God's Sake, lest he shou'd be flying off in ANOTHER *whirlwind*! There is little to be expected of improvement from a man at the age of thirty . . .

P.S. He said it was madness and that next to *Sally* he adored *Maria*!

Mrs Siddons heaved a sigh. She looked up. How happy could she be with neither!

P.P.S. Oh! that Caprice and Passion should thus obscure the many excellencies and lofty genius of this man!

Sarah Siddons put an end to Lawrence's nightmare of trying to be in two places at once, by herself going to Clifton to the bed-sides of her two beloved invalids. Much as she had dreaded finding the alteration in her Maria's face, she was quite unprepared to find her Sally in a glassy daze.

For Sally had become for the time being the iller of the two sisters. Indeed, in our own, more brutal age, odds might have been laid on which sister would stay the short course longer. Then, too, Sally was treated with laudanum in quantities sufficient to produce unconsciousness for considerable periods. But soon she had recovered enough to guide her quill pen through the briefest of notes to Miss Bird:

Thank heaven dear Maria's mind is perfectly tranquil concerning you know who! She thinks not of him, or if she does it is only to hope that I will never have anything to do with *our common enemy*, as she calls him.

Though if this sentiment of Maria's is what it would seem to be on the surface, or if she was inspired by a feeling that if she could not catch Lawrence she intended that her sister should not win him, is a matter for the charitable-minded reader to decide.

Poor ailing Maria—they moved her in a sedan chair from Mrs Pennington's to a lodging house on the opposite side of the square, and here is Sally writing to Miss Bird again:

She is now entirely confin'd to her own room, and yesterday cou'd not leave her bed. My Mother and I sit by her all day: she takes great quantities of laudanum which keep her in a continual stupor. I read to her, by her desire, almost constantly, for tho' she does not know what I read for five minutes together, she likes the sound while she is dozing upon her pillow. She is quite ignorant of her danger, nor does she seem to know she is in a Consumption, but thinks it some nervous spasmodic complaint which may be tedious, but not fatal.

In his next letter to Mrs Pennington Lawrence let fall a clear indication, at least to hindsight, of a faint inclination to return to an earlier attachment.

. . . In a very few days I suppose all Maria's sufferings will be at an end, and she will go where infancy and age are, but rarely *manhood* . . .

Dear, dear Mrs Siddons! She must be worn to nothing. I am almost thinking of writing to her . . .

Maria died on October 7th, 1798. There is a marble tablet still in the Parish Church of St Andrew's:

> In the Vault of this
> Church lies interred
> Maria Siddons
> aged 19

The Poet Young, in his *Night Thoughts*, unknowingly supplied her epitaph:

> Early, bright, transient, chaste as morning dew,
> She sparkled, was exhaled, and went to heaven.

The months went by. They served only to increase Sally's steadfast but distant devotion to Lawrence, whose weather-vane affections were veering again in another, an equally forbidden direction. But Sally shall tell her own sorry tale.

Writing on Christmas Eve, 1800, to Miss Bird she says:

... You may have heard, and it is true, of Mr L. being in Mrs Kemble's Box, and with my adorable Mama. I fancy she often sees him at the Theatre, but you have indeed been misinformed by those who told you he was ever of *our party*. All I see of him is now and then at the Theatre, when he just appears for a minute, as if *purposely* to make me a formal bow, and then he generally goes away, to some other part of the house, I suppose, and scarcely ever misses a night when my beautiful Mama performs, when he generally pays her a visit in her dressing-room. This I hear, not from my Mama, for unless I force her to it she never mentions him.

Again, in January 1801, Sally takes up her quill and eases her heart by unburdening it to Miss Bird:

. . . I confess the last time I saw him I made him as distant a Curtsy as he made me a Bow. I know my fascinating Mama sees him often, and I know she cannot cease to look on him with the partiality she always did, and always, I believe will feel for him, yet she never mentions him to me, never tells me he has spoken of me, or desires to be remembered to me — perhaps indeed he never *does* think or speak of me — but can I ever forget the days that are past? However *right* I may think it that we are separated, I would not have him *forget me*! . . . As for my *heart, it is a true and constant one*. I believe it *incapable* of change.

Poor Sally.

I sing but little now [she writes], and indeed I think *all* my energy is weaken'd since I have ceas'd to give delight to the three Beings who were dearest to me on earth: one is gone for ever, the second is *as though dead to me*, and the third no longer takes the same delight in me that once she did.

Within a year poor loving Sally, too, was dead.
Lawrence died in 1830 — the same year as Mrs Siddons. Lawrence, however, died of "Ossification of the heart" — hard hearted, then, to the end.

BOOK THREE

"Lord, give me chastity and continence—
but not yet."

The Confessions of St Augustine

◦❧ Chapter 1 ❧◦

" 'TWILL do."

A tall woman, majestic, dressed all in black, was standing, an immaculate figure of mourning, on the steps of Number 27, Upper Baker Street, overlooking the Regent's Park. A rusty black cottage-loaf of an old lady with, yes, a gleam in her eye, stood, puffing but respectable, beside her. The taller of the two turned to survey the elegant cream façade of Number 27 again: " 'Twill do well enough," she said.

"First Floor Front, Caesura—that will be a treat when the young ladies hold their dances."

"Hush, oh hush, Betsy. Your wits are wandering. I have but one daughter left to comfort me—and for me to comfort." The taller, more elegant, of the two bit her inflamed lips. For some years she had been suffering intermittently from the erysipelas which, in the end, would cause her proud spirit to submit to life's last diapason.

"Poor dear Mrs Siddons!" wrote Mrs Piozzi of Streatham to

F

her friend Mrs Pennington of Bristol. "She is never well long enough together. Always *some* torment, body or mind or both."

"One sweet daughter," repeated the taller lady, "to be my comfort and my gauge to Fate. And, of course, our dear little Future Patentee, Patty Wilkinson, to keep us both in spirits."

For the former "Wandering Patentee" Tate Wilkinson, last met firmly anchored at the Theatre Royal, Leeds, had sent at her urgent request his daughter to keep Cecilia Siddons company.

"Patty Nose-in-air," muttered the rounder of the two ladies. The more statuesque of the ladies pretended not to hear. She looked up to the fashionable balcony with the convoluted iron balustrade: " 'Twill do perfectly well when I have added to it the studio Mr Nash has promised to design for me."

"Him!" It was clear that Betsy Noakes held the distinguished architect in no higher regard than Patty Wilkinson. "New-fangled Jerry-builder."

Sarah Siddons affected not to hear, again. She turned to the sacking-wrapped bundle of womanhood whose breath was heavy with gin; presumably she was the caretaker. "Consider the business concluded, my good soul." Her good soul bobbed an abbreviated curtsy. "Here's for your pains — alms for oblivion" — and would herself have thrown in from force of habit, "Caesura", had not Betsy butted in ahead of her. Really Nannie could be very tiresome and wilful these days. But there was still her sweet Cecilia to be kept out of mischief when she herself was busy with her biography.

Her biography! Stiff and inflamed as her lips might be, a faint smile touched them momentarily at the thought.

So it was on the steps of Number 27, Upper Baker Street, that Mrs Siddons' biographer waited to be admitted one April day, some years later. His shoulders were bent, his steel-rimmed glasses crooked, his coat snuff-stained; in fact he looked generally scruffy and every inch a scholar. No prize is offered for identifying James Boaden (back from teaching The Skipper's little daughter how to handle a pair of oars—the better to bear her father companee. That lass was brighter at her oars than at her Latin declensions—strange).

Our worthy stage historian had not been able to resist writing the Definitive Siddons (Sarah). The fact that neither could Mr Poet and Historian Campbell had not yet been divulged to him. Nor had James Boaden's efforts to capture the genius of Mrs Siddons and transfix it to the page been revealed to Mr Poet and Historian Campbell.

Save for the agonising rash on her face which caused her to retire from the vulgar gaze when in the recurrent throes of her complaint, Mrs Siddons was as fascinating, at least to James Boaden, as ever. It was just as Mrs Piozzi of Streatham so often said:

> Dear Charming Siddons keeps her empire over all hearts still . . . poor dear pretty Siddons. What *has* she been doing to her mouth? In true sadness, what *can* be the matter with her lips? Lips that never were equalled in communication of tenderness or sublimity! Dear Soul, what can ail her? She dreamed, once, that all her teeth came out upon the stage . . .

And was it not as Mrs Piozzi's friend the great sage, Dr Johnson, wrote to her: "Mrs Siddons is unspoilt by the two powerful corruptions of mankind: Praise and Money." Of praise the great actress had had no stint. Money she had had to earn.

Her fine bones, even in age, saved her face and gave to it an indestructible beauty. There was nothing of her pert niece Fanny's description of her aunt, "a magnificent ruin tottering to its fall," in James Boaden's eyes. No hatchet job for him.

Take this morning, for instance. A handful of years had

drifted through those still lovely fingers, since she had removed to Number 27. Indeed by now the greatest tragic actress of her day—who knows, perhaps of our own day, too—had retired from the boards and was at work on her biography with Boaden. Today she seemed reluctant to discuss her Irish trips, and dwelt rather on her last appearance—The Lady. Boaden let her run on.

"I do agree with Mr Hazlitt," Mrs Siddons was saying. "Not of course in all things—my sleep-walking scene, for instance." She quoted balefully: "When she declaims, 'I tell you, he cannot rise from his grave,' she repeats the action with both hands sawing the air in the style of parliamentary oratory, the worst of all others."

James Boaden threw up his hands and sawed the air too.

"No, indeed," Mrs Siddons settled back in her Sheraton. "But it is when he says, 'Players should be immortal, if their own wishes or ours could make them so. They not only die like other people, but they grow old like other people.'"

"I deny that! I'd like to take that fellow Hazlitt out at dawn," James Boaden added darkly. Absently he picked up his plume and made a pass or so.

Mrs Siddons smiled gently. Her whole countenance, her whole being, was miraculously touched to tenderness. "Nay," she said, "it is the common lot. Players are not exempt from it. They can be no longer themselves as we have known them, even while living. Take my poor Sid, my late husband. Sid died suddenly, as he had prayed to die, without a sigh."

James Boaden sighed for him.

"Yet," said Mrs Siddons, "we had to part some years before —age and pain had made him so intolerant. But once, when I was nobbut a slip of a girl, as Betsy Noakes would say, I did adore him. Ay, me!"

Ay, her, indeed.

Mrs Siddons came back from the past. "Since I have left the stage," she admitted, "from the want of excitement I have never been happy." A clock chimed its silver hour. "Oh, dear," she sighed, "this is the time I used to be thinking of going to the theatre."

James Boaden consulted his own chronometer. "Quite so," he said.

"First came the pleasure of dressing for my part, and then," her eyes sparkled, "the pleasure of acting it. And my public—they treated me like a Queen."

"If one were to ask me, 'What is a Queen?' I should say, 'Mrs Siddons'," Boaden declared.

"Do you remember my last appearance? In the Lady?" The question was unnecessary.

"Do I remember!" Boaden announced with considerable relish. "There was something idolatrous about your reception."

"The crowd was immense!"

"It would be. It should be."

"It was."

"My sleep-walking scene was considered so shattering that the audience stood on the benches to demand that the Scottish Tragedy should end with that scene. The curtain," said the divine Sarah, with considerable satisfaction—indeed, had she been one jot less than divine, erysipelas or not, she could have been said to smirk, "was then lowered for twenty minutes."

"And when it arose once more," James Boaden prompted her.

"I was discovered sitting at a table, dressed all in white. I came forward in the midst of a perfect thunderstorm of applause. Silence being obtained, I recited an address. It ended, I remember so well:

> Herself, subdu'd, resigned the melting spell,
> And breathes, with swelling heart, her long,
>   her last, farewell.

"Was it not there I concluded the lines?" the Queen of Tragedy questioned her biographer keenly.

But James Boaden was in tears.

There was no knock at the door. In trundled Betsy Noakes. One look at the pair of them sufficed her: "Now, Master Jaimie, don't you go over-exciting Miss Sarah beyond her strength," she admonished the distinguished biographer, set down the tay-tray, and waddled off.

James Boaden blew his nose.

"And now," he said, "for Ireland."

"Not now," said Mrs Siddons. "Tomorrow. Tomorrow is another day." And suddenly she was an old lady sitting still; her hands folded in her lap; an old lady touched by serenity that experience can bring like a blessing to some women, and with hope for the tomorrows to come.

And like the chimes of Time's own clock, tomorrow did come, to be succeeded by tomorrow and tomorrow, in each of which James Boaden tried to brace himself to ask Sarah Siddons a delicate question. A very delicate question.

"They tell me, 'tis common talk about the town, that Mistress Piozzi is declaring that you make your age older by ten summers than the true reaping of the years. Why?"

"Why? I warrant you will not find many women with the wit to do likewise," Mrs Siddons' left eyelid blinked—in anyone less majestic it could have been described as a wink. "It is common knowledge that whenever a lady of uncertain age is asked how old she is, the poor, foolish soul deducts ten years; she had much better add ten years to her age, for then the impertinent questioner goes on his way thinking, 'Ah, there's a fine old woman for you!'" And had it not been bruited abroad that la Siddons had no vestige of a sense of humour, James Boaden could have sworn that there was a gleam of fun in her eyes. Or could it be that his steel-rimmed spectacles were crooked?

Day after day, they sat there in an upper room, looking into the Regent's Park; Boaden trying to edge his illustrious subject into Ireland, as it were, and Sarah Siddons shying away like a high-mettled horse. Today, though, he had screwed his courage to the sticking point.

"And now," he said, with more bravura than he felt, "let us attack your visits to," he coined a phrase, "the—um—Emerald Isle," and affected not to see her arresting gesture.

"My first visit," Mrs Siddons specified. She settled back as far as the forbidding Sheraton would allow, and squared her massive shoulders. Mrs Siddons was no slouch. "My husband was alive then and went ahead to satisfy my contract. It was the first time I had set foot on the sliding sea. I had never felt the Majesty of The Divine Creator so fully before."

"Ah!" said Boaden. This was something like!

"I was so dreadfully sea-sick!"

"Oh," said Boaden. This was not going to look at all poetic in the hindsight of history, but, a conscientious quiller, he noted down the unfortunate fact. Worse was to follow.

"After a storm-driven passage through waves as high as mountains, the rain came bucketing down and instead of being driven to a comfortable and comforting inn, I and Betsy Noakes, who was of course a part of my *équipe*—she was a youngish woman then—we were obliged to spend an hour and a half—enough time for her to take me through some half dozen new prologues and a few exceptionally difficult epilogues—consigned in the dreariest dungeon of the Custom's House."

Her biographer's quill was racing. "And after that?" he urged.

"Oh, after that—I shall never forget it—we were forced to tramp the wet streets with not so much as a drum to hold off the torrential rain, seeking some—any—shelter; and this at two o'clock in the morning!"

Her biographer, shocked, and this not for the first time, clicked his tongue.

"Aye," said Sarah. "And if you ask me the Irish Capital City is a Sink of Iniquity and other filthiness—or so it seemed to me the first time I was to visit it."

"And the second time?"

Sarah smiled. "Ah," she said, "that was different. But the first time, don't ye know, that first time when Betsy and I knocked at one of many doors, the landlady, on hearing that I was an actress, took it for granted that Betsy and I were in search of a brothel, in which to ply."

"A . . . a . . . a . . ."

"Brothel," said Sarah Siddons roundly. "She told us that it was contrary to her rule to entertain ladies at her brothel, which was a respectable whorehouse. You should have seen Betsy's face." And she went off into a peal of laughter. "Rosalind," Boaden identified, even though there was the crackle of dead leaves in the *voix d'or*.

"From that moment I took against the Irish—most of 'em— all ostentation and insincerity! And as to their sense of finery . . ." Mrs Siddons looked at the ceiling. "They are very like the French."

"Very like, very like."

"But," said Sarah, "not so cleanly."

James Boaden sniffed.

"And then they are tenacious of their country as to a degree of folly that is laughable." She gave another girlish peal of silvery laughter. The bells were cracked.

James Boaden did not join in. His thoughts had drifted off to no-longer merry old John Philip Kemble, whose biography he tackled on Sarah's off afternoons. For was it not in Dublin's Fair City, where, he was reliably informed, the gals were so pretty, singing cockles and mussels alive, alive-o! that a repellent gallery-goer had sung out: "Johnny honey, there's the least taste in life of yez shirt got out behind yez". He pulled himself together. It would never do to drift off to sleep in The Presence.

"However, all's well that ends well. The Bard," Mrs Siddons was saying. "For in little more than ten weeks I made one thousand pounds out of the Irish Admiration of my Art." The old lady preened. So might a well-pleased eagle fluff out its plumes.

"Well done!" James Boaden encouraged his subject. "Well done indeed!"

"In fact by the year I call my Galindo Summer I had paid no less than six visits to Ireland, and all of them highly profitable." She rubbed skeletal hands together. So did her biographer. The pair of them rubbed and beamed in a pause that would have done Harold Pinter's great, great, and again great, grandfather credit.

At length Mrs Siddons returned to her muttons. "On that very first visit to . . ." she sought for the right word, rejected one or two that occurred to her, then settled for "Erin".

"Two Rs?" enquired Boaden.

"Two," boomed Sarah Siddons — "I think."

Boaden tried it out. His quill protested. Both ways looked wrong.

"Our manager, Richard Daly, of Castle Daly, was no gentleman where pretty and poor young actresses were concerned."

James Boaden clucked.

"But he had won a reputation for paying his company to the last groat."

"Groat," scratched the quill.

"He was a man of good family, and," a gleam came momentarily into the monumental Mrs Siddons' eye, "but for a squint, very good-looking."

"Pity about that squint," said Boaden.

"No matter," Sarah said. "It did not stop him from making his star — me —" she pointed out, "and Sid, my husband, acquainted with the Right People."

"So important," said James Boaden. "I remember when I was tutor to Lord Melbourne's illegitimate . . ."

"Enough!" said Sarah Siddons, and she put an end to the interview.

"But," James Boaden was about to plead, when he looked up. Sarah Siddons, her work done, was nodding. *Et tu* Sarah!

❧ Chapter 2 ❧

IT is a truth universally acknowledged that the poet and
cleric, John Donne, was apt to be right in whatever point
he chose to make in his excellently chiselled prose. His
letter to Sir T. Lucy bears out, roughly, the rule: "I take account
that the writing of letters is a kind of ecstasy and a suspension
of the soul which doth then communicate itself to two bodies."

But there could be notable exceptions.

One of these is when the letter in question contains the
sinister suggestion: "A person so long eminent as you for your
public talents and *supposed private virtues*." Moreover when the
letter is printed in an eighty-four-page pamphlet, priced at
five shillings a copy—an important expenditure in those days—
and when the personage so addressed is the nonpareil of tragedi-
ennes, the Great Mrs Siddons, whose fame puts the centuries
to shame, and the writer, a Mrs Catherine Galindo (Formerly
Kitty Gough), a poor, low, clumsy actress, known to audiences
in Bath and Belfast as "Sepulchral Gough" whom, hindsight

suggests, was indeed a wronged wife, the fusing of soul, in the sense that John Donne uses it, does not apply.

As could be foreseen, many a session and many a month had passed before Mrs Siddons allowed James Boaden to edge her into her second visit to Ireland. Seasons came and seasons went, each one lending a different aspect to the Regent's Park. But at length she embraced the idea of reliving her last folly. "I was in my early middle-age, well, only forty-eight, in my Galindo summer."

"Gal-in-do," scratched her biographer. "What initial?" For James Boaden prided himself on his attention to detail.

"Initial? I called Galindo—Galindo, such a musical name! And then he was a trifle younger than I. But after sorrow and darkness life was suddenly a shining delight once more. Patty Wilkinson, who accompanied me, was like an elder daughter, or a younger sister to me. Sweet Putty, she was patti in my hands. I mean . . ."

"Mercy on us! Not so fast," Boaden pleaded, his steel-rimmed spectacles steaming up. "You have left me far behind, my friend, far behind." Actually he was spidering a note to himself: "N.B. Young Galindo, whatever his initial, was half her age and he could have been her son!"

"I admit it was a folly," Mrs Siddons was saying. "A folly born of my ripeness and my misery."

"A madness," her quiller was quilling.

And Mrs Siddons? She had turned her one-time penetrating gaze far, far away through the fresh green boughs of the Regent's Park, where she discerned her earlier self, a stripling girl—well, a young woman of a mere forty-eight summers, madly in love with a broth of a boy of four-and-twenty, while her biographer nodded into his inkwell.

Patty Wilkinson, it seemed, was a prime cause of the affaire Galindo. It happened thus.

[172]

Patty had met and, being young, became quite dazzled by Sepulchral Gough, who had, by means of sheer persistence, achieved an engagement at one of her father's Theatres — Walking-understudy and "utility player" — in out-of-season Bath. Sepulchral Gough, who knew which side her bread might, with luck and by candlelight, be buttered, made much of the Guv'nor's daughter.

Galindo, dark, slender and dashing, was passing for a fencing master at Bath. Being a young man of no particular ambition, at that time, beyond that of being kept out-of-work, he noted the energy, misplaced though it might be, of la Gough. She would do, he conceded, for the time being. Thus, Sepulchral Gough became Sepulchral Galindo.

Now it so happened that Mrs Siddons was, at that time, combining a dutiful visit to her ailing husband at Bath with persuading the Tate Wilkinsons to lend their charming Patty to be a playmate in the school holidays to her only surviving daughter, Cecilia, and a close companion to herself during term for a season or so. "Poor pretty Siddons," Mrs Piozzi was writing, when news of la Siddons' new companion buzzed its way out to Tooting Bec. "Poor pretty Siddons, I think she is not happy in her children. The elder son *will* be a strolling Player. The second has bad eyes, almost to blindness. The pretty daughters both are dead, poor things, and *my* God-child, named Cecilia after *my* sweet daughter, is spoiled and fretful."

While Sarah Siddons' *pour-parlers* were taking place on Patty's immediate future — the advantages of her spending the London season under the illustrious wings weighed against her absence from the Maternal hearth, wherever it was set up, for by now the well-known Patentee, her Pa, had Theatres Royal in several important Provincial cities — Patty took time by the fore-lock by introducing her famous friend to her infamous friend, and the Galindos moved in, as it were, on Sarah Siddons, which is to say that quickly they took up their skirmishing positions in readiness for richly rewarding campaigning.

Ah, the delights of the giddy days that followed, days in which the all-too-evidently smitten Sarah decided to revive her Hamlet:

> About this period [ran Sepulchral Galindo's scurrilous letter] you proposed to perform Hamlet, *for no other purpose than to be taught Fencing* by Mr G. for by so doing you had an excuse to have him constantly with you, to the exclusion of *my* company, for you said you could not be instructed while any person looked on.

Aware of the need to keep la Galindo if not sweet, at least not overtly sour, Sarah even stooped to promise her a season with jolly John Philip's London Company, when it reassembled in Covent Garden—to the jolly one's fury, as their old friend Mrs Inchbald revealed:

> He came to me like a madman. Said Mrs Siddons had been imposed upon by persons it was a disgrace to her to *know*, and he begged *me* to explain this to her—even to be familiar with such people was a lack of virtue.

Sepulchral Galindo's London engagement whistled down the wind. But Covent Garden having closed its doors against her she found a perch at the Smock Alley playhouse in Dublin, and smartly whisked her man over the water, with Sarah following in hot pursuit and Patty Wilkinson in tow.

"Then Patty Wilkinson was, as it were, your Cicerone," observed Boaden, much relieved. Even a very young Cicerone being better, in his eyes, than no Cicerone at all.

Mrs Siddons inclined her head. "A Respectable Thespian must be seen to be Respectable."

"Quite so," said Boaden. Any loss of reputation to the divine Siddons would be a loss to the whole world, he felt. He said so. "Hallelujah," ejaculated Mrs Siddons so loudly that she made him jump.

A wasted afternoon at Number 27.

"Miss Sairey's gotten out of the hay the wrong way," Nannie Noakes warned Master Boaden. The patient biographer resigned to absenting himself from the Em'rald Isle, caesura, and to filling in by the Q and A method—that is if he could get any A's from Mrs Siddons.

Mrs Siddons had just been expressing herself on the subject of the Late Mrs Bracegirdle. "Not that I have the requisite years at my recall actually to have seen her act."

"Quite so," Boaden sounded deferential. "And what is your opinion of Young Master Betty?"

"Him!" said Mrs Siddons and had she been any day-to-day Thespian one might be pardoned for thinking that she sniffed. As it was, Boaden settled for "she inhaled deeply".

"That little scene-sneaker—all socks and smirks! That Baby-face who has not even the elements of an actor about him. That . . . That . . ." words failed her but only for a moment. "I never could abide Infant phenomenons," she remembered her own early appearances. She switched horses. "You should hear what Mr M'Cready has to say of the inattentive little chatterbox—Never on time at rehearsals. And so on and," she bethought herself, "so on."

James Boaden looked at the ceiling. "Betty late than never," he observed.

He blushed.

That very night, as though to make up for a sultry afternoon, there came a knock at James Boaden's Bloomsbury lodging so handy for a quick dive into the British Museum one foggy day in London Town. Boaden, candle in hand, peered out into the obscure night. There, swaying slightly on his landlady's doorstep stood two Sisters of the Night. One would have been plenty.

"My name," said the fatter of the two, "is Kezia Quicktobed."

"And I," said the taller of the two, "am Salubria Golightly."

"We've come to tell you about Sairey Siddons."

They refreshed themselves from a bottle of gin, swig and swig about, recollected their manners, offered Boaden a swig while he recollected his wits and refused. Kezia thumped the cork in.

"Mrs Siddons?"

"In Ireland."

"For a price!" they said as one.

James Boaden blinked. Something—some memory evoked by those tawdry swaying figures caught in the leaping flame of his candle, was drawing him back to his boyhood. He had beheld those grimy faces before, but where?

"A fair price," the taller of the two with the bedraggled scarlet plumes in her rusty black-straw bonnet, invited.

"A *good* price," her slightly more gin-sodden friend without any bonnet at all but with a soiled pink rose in her hair, intimated.

"I am sure we can arrive at an agreement as to proper remuneration for a fully authenticated account of whatever it may be you have come to tell me." The snuffy old bird in the carpet slippers shuffled them, sputtering even more candlegrease over his dressing-gown and nearly setting himself alight, to boot. His visitors took counsel of each other and the gin-bottle. Thus fortified they followed the old goose through the dark hall smelling of the ghosts of cabbage dinners, onwards and upwards, and at length came to the fourth floor back, as his landlady, Miss Hardtimes, who had seen better days, but not much, called his little kingdom. His two visitors plumped themselves, unasked, on to his bed. The fat trollop took a refreshing swig. "I was in need of that!" The tall trollop snatched and swigged, too, "Not much left—still . . ." Generously she offered the dregs to her host, who fended them off with an inky claw. "Now, ladies, one at a time."

"Money first," they said, as one.

"Money," repeated the old bird with the skew-wiff spectacles — where was it they had seen those spectacles before?

"Money on the table where I can keep an eye on it. I will hear your story before remuneration." So lovingly did he dwell on the syllables that almost he might have been the old Shakespearean clown.

"Oughter be ashamed of 'erself."

"Show off."

"Always was and always will be."

"*And* no better than she should be."

"She was brought up proper though, was our Sairey—"

"Madam Kemble did 'er level best for 'er, I will say."

"So did Betsy Noakes."

"Many's the slapped bum she's had from Betsy."

"Stop! . . . Stop! . . . Stop! . . . You . . ." Boaden pointed an inky finger at the fat one, "must be Kezia! And you," he pointed to the tall slut, "must be Salubria."

"Like we told you! Don't you never listen when you're told things?"

"Ireland," commanded Mrs Siddons' biographer pointing to the money on the table. "Come back to Erin," he insisted.

◄ Chapter 3 ►

A MORE rewarding afternoon at Number 27. Sarah Siddons, as though to make amends for her last session with James Boaden, went straight to her Galindo Summer without further guidance from her biographer.

"Such happy, happy days — sweet Patty Wilkinson with her great friend, Mrs Galindo, and so, in order that I should not be too solitary, Mr Galindo took me driving in the dearest little conveyance — he said it was his wife's favourite equipage."

"Indeed," said her biographer. He was to hear more about these outings *à deux*.

"I had then a curricle," wrote Galindo's much-tried wife in her wickedest vein, "I requested you might use my little carriage as if it were your own; you took me at my word, for from that time I was entirely excluded from it!"

"Such days," repeated Mrs Siddons; and something of their

ecstasy lingered in her voice, her eyes, her manner. "The sun shone as never before or since, and the afternoons—those afternoons"—words failed her. Not so sepulchral Galindo.

You accepted a contract to play at Limerick and Cork. You went in the curricle with Mr G. and travelled with him the rest of the day, arriving some hours after Miss Wilkinson and myself.

Mrs Siddons came back from her day dream. "Happy days, happy days!" Clearly, having once embarked for Cythera, she was enjoying embarking for it all over again.

Boaden's quill spidered away but could scarcely keep up with his subject.

And far away in distant Tooting Bec another quill was spidering too. "Dear! Charming! Excellent! Admirable Mrs Siddons—ever on the wing to something that calls her to Distant Regions—Scotland or *Ireland*."

As the Siddons seasons in Cork and Limerick proceeded and Sarah kept her endearing Galindo at her side whether his sepulchral wife was "giving" at the playhouses or not, la Galindo grew, understandably enough, increasingly vituperative in the privacy of the Marriage bed: "I became very unhappy, and expressed my dissatisfaction to Mr G."

Poor Playboy of the Western World, caught in a web woven between two furies. At length an engagement was secured for the Sepulchral One in Belfast while Mrs Siddons was appearing in Dublin. Mrs Siddons' Galindo Summer, it transpired, was to prolong itself not solely to the Winter of Mrs Galindo's Discontent, but to seven such winters.

"Destitute of all those advantages which you possess I have been your victim now, for seven miserable years."

[179]

Seven years for Rachel has a Biblical ring to it, but seven years to get her own back from Sarah Siddons? Seven years in which three unequal souls knotted together seemingly inextricably, by a tangle of fate, must have felt like doom to the injured wife.

It was as though your passion for Mr G. had overcome all considerations of propriety. You never suffered *him* to be from your side—he spent *all day and half the night with you*, returning home at one, two, or even *three in the morning*. Provoked beyond all patience by such conduct I remonstrated in the warmest manner to Mr G.

After these apparently well-justified complaints the injured wife stooped to sinister innuendo: "You were very ill for about a week. *The exact nature of your illness I am ignorant of.*"

"Of course you took this reprehensible creature before the Courts of Justice over that disgraceful slander," said James Boaden, deeply shocked.

"That I did not," Mrs Siddons said, rather mildly for her. "I would not trouble my Man of Law with such a trifle."

"A trifle, you call it? Madam, you astonish me." This was the nearest thing to a reproach that Boaden could ever bring himself to make to the incomparable Sarah Siddons.

Skip a page or so of the eighty-four odd—at times very odd—pamphlet and we shall come to the daunting threat: "I shall now, Madam, pause to make a few observations on your conduct as it appeared to me, ignorant as I then was of the *shameful truth*."

At insinuation Mrs Galindo can have had few rivals along the laser-beam of history.

"On your return to England you *constantly* wrote to Mr G. and *sometimes* to me. Your letters to me were filled with the most unbounded expressions of friend-ship."

What then, we might ask ourselves, can the letters to Mr G. have been like? But answer comes there none. Can Hindsight, alongside antique Homer, nod?

Sepulchral Galindo next sounds the Wagnerian theme of the paucity of terms offered her for a season at Covent Garden —clearly before John Philip had put the heavy Kemble foot down on her engagement, the offer which, in his absence abroad, had been secured for her at Mrs Siddons' insistence. ". . . Compared with their usual terms, a very indifferent offer."

And the sniff with which this complaint was no doubt concluded, echoes down the centuries. She went on—how she went on—to complain of John Philip's changed attitude towards her Art when he latterly went over to Dublin, where, possibly as walking-understudy, she had already inherited sundry small parts.

I had known your brother for many years and he had always behav'd to me with the utmost propriety. On this occasion his conduct was the very reverse. Nothing could exceed his rudeness. He was resolved to force me to resign my engagement. I demanded an explanation.

It seems he was only too willing to supply reasons why she should not appear on the same stage on which he himself was "giving", and why she would not be to the London public's taste.

"He affected a vast deal of candour."

Galindo, having arrived in London ahead of his wife, Mrs Siddons instructed Patty Wilkinson to write to Mrs Galindo on her behalf advising her to stay in Ireland. We can believe that such communications between bosom friends were not received without painful emotion and, in Mrs Galindo's case, spite predominated. She made for London without further loss of time.

Shortly after these events Sarah Siddons removed from Westbourne Grove to Hampstead, where she fell ill again.

"There," Mrs Galindo accuses her. "Mr G. was your constant visitor, and as *he* could sleep upon a sopha in your parlour he always stayed at night."

"Dear me, dear me, dear me, dear Lady," clucked James Boaden. "Whatever will History make of that?"

Three years flew after the manner that years do, when they do not lag, in which Mrs Siddons remained at the mercy of her passion for the Married Man young enough to be her son. And then, in an evil hour, a Mr M'Cready, by overbidding everyone else, obtained the lease of the New Manchester Theatre.

We hearing he wanted a partner, Mr G. wrote to him, saying he wish'd to work with him. The money demanded was three thousand and five hundred pounds. Mr G. saw so many advantages that he agreed to pay the whole sum over a period of one year and six months; a thousand pounds being demanded on signature, another thousand this day month, the remaining three payments of five hundred pounds at six months each.

Of course it was impossible for the Church Mice Galindos to call on two thousand pounds at such short — or indeed at any — notice. Galindo turned to Mrs Siddons to lend him one thousand pounds. The besotted Sarah agreed, subject to its being kept from her ailing husband's ears and with the proviso that he should repay her as soon as he could.

Could anything be more repugnant to the jealous and envious married woman?

"You know, Madam, the reluctance I felt at any further *seeming* obligation to you but I was forced to give way."

Nevertheless a bond was executed in the name of Patty Wilkinson, since "Mrs Siddons did not want her husband to know".

Boaden looked upset as these details were laid before him. It was going to look black—very black. Centuries would not whiten this little deed.

"I forbade that . . . that woman—ever to let me see her face again."

"Dear me, yes—I mean, dear me, no," said the shocked biographer.

As might easily be foretold, the partnership of M'Cready and Galindo soon foundered, and a sort of financial This-is-the-house-that-Jack-built took place in reverse; for M'Cready had not the money to refund to Galindo, who had not the money to repay Mrs Siddons, who dared not tell her by this time dying husband.

Among the many insults hurled at Mrs Siddons from Sepulchral Galindo's shrill pamphlet was the accusation that she had stayed on in Ireland although she had been told that her daughter Sally was dying: "What sort of Mother lingers on in dalliance while her *supposedly* beloved daughter coughs her life away?"

And if a sepulchral voice could screech as well as boom we can be sure that Mrs Galindo's wrathful range embraced the gamut.

Seven years of suspicion, followed by horrid certainty, followed by jealousy, followed by all-consuming rage were packed into that pamphlet.

"It is a wonder that I had any public left when that virago had done with my reputation," said the old lady, sitting if anything more upright than ever.

"Your achievement should obliterate such revilings," said her biographer.

Nothing for it but to walk home through the park to calm

his nerves when the session was over. And this James Boaden did. No blinking it away, his beloved, incomparable Mrs Siddons had been very foolish—very foolish indeed. Confound that Galindo Summer.

◄ Chapter 4 ►

As Sarah Siddons' life drew, at seventy-six, to its slow close, what can she have felt? Exhaustion certainly, for she had lived fully, loved fitfully, acted greatly, borne children, seen those she loved die, and if seventy-six is no great age in our own day, it was a time to wither in that in which she lived. In spite of age and retirement—several retirements— a restlessness must have possessed her, heritage of her candlelit and footlight days in which she had trod the boards from Barn to Theatre Royal and always to the acclaim of the lowest to the highest in the land.

She made, in the critic Hazlitt's wise eyes, the cardinal mistake of returning to play her Lady Macbeth for this charity or that occasion for some years after she had left the stage. How his measured words must have disturbed and dismayed her.

Writing in general of the common lot of players too old to play, in an essay addressed to Mrs Siddons, this great assayer of the art of acting said:

Their health, strength, beauty, voice, fail them; nor can they, without these advantages, perform the same feats [most bitter words to read] or command the applause that they did . . . Mrs Siddons retired once from the stage, why should she return again? She cannot retire from it twice with dignity . . . She raised Tragedy to the skies. It was something above Nature. Power was seated on her brow. Passion emanated from her breast as from a shrine. Her voice had been as though a trumpet had awakened the sleeping and the dead. Is she to continue on the stage till, all her grace and all her grandeur gone, shall leave behind her only a Melancholy blank? . . .

Mrs Siddons always spoke as slow as she ought; she now speaks slower than she did. "The line took labours and the words move slow." There is too long a pause between each sentence and between each word in each sentence. [Caesura?]

Ah! how the emptied husk of Mrs Siddons must have regretted the years that had her by the heels.

She died at her house beside the Regent's Park seventeen months after the painter Lawrence died.

Let us, in the words of Hazlitt, leave her to her repose.

* * *

. . . .The scene is Heaven. Two spirits have drifted into the same ambiance — Mrs Siddons and her biographer. They communicate.

The Spirit of James Boaden: Half your letters seemed to be dated from This Seat or 't other Castle.
Mrs Siddons (eagerly): And Rectory. Do not forget t' Rectory — before everything one was respectable!
The spirit of James Boaden looks at her, about to say something, opens his ghostly mouth, thinks better of it, and closes it again as the spirits drift apart.

⪥ Explanation ⪦

"A woman should never apologise; it makes a man feel insecure."
Probably Barbara Cartland

And so, instead of an apologia I will set out before the reader the philosophy of the Higher Truth.

The Higher Truth was defined by the Drama Critic, James Agate, and ever since I read that definition I have written in its light. But in order to expound upon the Higher Truth, I must enlarge first upon what is regarded as the normal truth.

What is truth? In spite of Biblical and Baconian precedent I beg the reader to stay for an answer. Truth, the ghost of Agate and I contend, is merely what actually happened; the Higher Truth is how it should have happened.

This biography, then, is largely a work of fiction—a novel—founded on fact. The fact is that there was, plumb in the middle of the eighteenth century and one third of the way through the nineteenth century, a celebrated tragic actress, unrivalled in her own days and quite possibly in ours, too, known as Mrs Siddons—the incomparable Sarah Siddons. She was born Sarah Kemble, the daughter of Roger and Sarah Kemble, Strolling Players, at an Inn in Brecon High Street: "The Shoulder of Mutton"; and this in itself was something of a refinement, for the Kembles were wont to drop their babies in the wings or in whatever barn they chanced to be storming as they strolled.

So much for history, then. A great deal of research was undertaken and—in the light of the higher truth—discarded. It took no time at all for me to invent the good Madam Kemble's irate Mother, putting back the gin in a higher sphere. Betsy Noakes, sometime member of the Kemble company and principal bottom-smacker to two generations of the Family and their Troupe, was one of the characters who sprang out live from somewhere in the regions of my diaphragm, while I was taking coffee at Fortnum and Mason's with a colleague, before ever I had started writing the text, and Betsy proceeded to write herself, as did a pair of urchins, born to be drabs, who sprang out of the names I found for them, Kezia and Salubria, two tatterdemalion brats with mothers in the Troupe.

Flushed with success, I went on to do far worse from the point of view of the lower truth. One of Mrs Siddons' contemporary biographers was a stage-struck quill-pusher named James Boaden. I started him off at an early age, a Barn-struck boy in crooked steel-rimmed spectacles, and later found him employment as tutor to the off-spring of well-known fictional characters, so that before long I manipulated him—or he, me—like one of my own invented characters.

To Mrs Siddons I have been most unfair. Once she grew up I disliked her, though I liked her enormously while she was a child. And this disapproval lasted until she became an old lady —a magnificent wreck tottering through the memories of a shameful *affaire* with a flashing Irish fencing master half her age.

I do not claim that I have captured her greatness — her incomparable achievement as an actress — who could? Is not a success in one leading role vastly like a success in another, which could only lead on to the reader's ennui, at least as set down by me? Other writers, other strengths.

About the story I wished to tell I was fairly clear from the outset — a condition most unusual in my work. It can be summed up as the three ages of Sarah Siddons.

First the child Stroller, keeping the rain off her hair-ribbons under a drum; a circumstance to which she attributed the Queenly carriage of her crowns.

Then the mother of two star-crossed daughters, Sally and Maria, both in love with the portrait painter Lawrence, with whom their mother was in love, too; both foredoomed to early deaths. This Sarah Siddons did not endear herself to me.

For Mrs Siddons in retirement — my third Siddonian plateau — I felt total compassion and not a little awe. It was in her old age that, for the first time, I had an affection for her.

I was cavalier and wilful in the manner that I cut away all the undergrowth of children and friends that tangled the way of the story I started out to tell, contenting myself, if no one else, by merely indicating her two sons and her other two daughters, one of whom died when a few months old in circumstances of not a little mystery — or was that a seventh child? The reader will readily recognise how vulnerable to error the mere truth leaves me.

Mr Siddons — Sarah's Sid — emerged briefly from the wings only to slip back into them when not needed on the voyage. I could not resist the grave Roman aspect of her brother, John Philip Kemble, and dubbed him Merry John Philip most of the time, much as one calls an unusually tall man "Tiny".

What else did I do? Well, for two things, I fused two Theatres Royal, the Theatre Royal Drury Lane and the Theatre Royal Covent Garden, mainly because in the eighteenth and early nineteenth centuries playhouses on fire always seemed to burn down to the ground and I save but a few charred remains where once tragedy and grandeur reigned.

The two fires with everything lost but the urge to act seemed to cry out for telescoping into one great blaze. Thus Mrs Siddons lost the lace she treasured, for it had once belonged to Marie-Antoinette, and she used it sparingly (in fact she reserved it for the *Winter's Tale* where, in the statue scene, she enveloped herself in it to form and soften the folds in the sculpted marble). This unique and carefully husbanded piece of historic lace I burned in the wrong conflagration.

Many years ago, when I was working with that brilliant humorist S. J. Simon, we wrote a highly unorthodox novel about Shakespeare—*No Bed for Bacon*. This we prefaced with

WARNING TO SCHOLARS
This book is fundamentally unsound.

One discerning critic, however (he must have had a forgiving soul), named Clifford Bax, declared in his critique of it that the book was only superficially unsound; beneath the surface it was indeed authentic.

Clearly he, too, perceived the Higher Truth of the characters.

AFTER-THOUGHT
The truth as things should have been comes also to soothe the conscience of the liar. For, after all, what is a lie if not an exercise of the Higher Truth?

❧ Bibliography ❧

Agate, James, ed., *The English Dramatic Critics*, Arthur Barker, 1932.

Appleton, William W., *Charles Macklin*, Oxford University Press, 1960.

D'Arblay, Madame (Fanny Burney), *Diaries and Letters*, Macmillan, 1904.

Bingham, Madeleine, *Sheridan. The Track of a Comet*, George Allen and Unwin, 1972.

Boaden, James, *The Life of John Philip Kemble, Volume Two*, 1825.

Boaden, James, *Memoirs of Mrs Siddons*, Gibbings and Co., 1827.

Brahms, Caryl and S. J. Simon, *No Nightingales*, 1944.

Campbell, Thomas, *Life of Mrs Siddons*, Effingham Wilson, 1834.

Clinton-Baddeley, V. C., *All Right on the Night*, G. P. Putnam, 1954.

Clunes, Alec, *The British Theatre*, Cassells, 1964.

The Annals of Covent Garden Theatre, 1732–1897, Wyndham, 1906.

Galinda, Letter to Mrs Siddons, (Pamphlet), 1809.

Garlick, Kenneth, *Sir Thomas Lawrence*, Routledge and Kegan Paul, 1952.

Haydon, *Autobiography and Journals*, Macdonald, 1950 (first published 1853).

Hazlitt, W., *Criticism and Dramatic Essays*, Routledge and Kegan Paul, 1851.

Kemble, Frances Anne (Fanny Kemble), *Record of a Girlhood*, Richard Bentley and Son, 1878.

Knapp, *The Artist's Love Story told in the Letters of Sir Thomas Lawrence, Mrs Siddons and her daughters*, George Allen and Unwin, 1904.

Manvell, Roger, *Sarah Siddons*, Heinemann, 1970.

Parsons, Mrs Clement, *The Incomparable Siddons*, Methuen, 1909.

Intimate Letters of Hester Piozzi and Mrs Penelope Pennington, John Lane, 1914.

Royde-Smith, Naomi, *The Private Life of Mrs Siddons*, Gollancz, 1933.

Russell, W. Clarke, *Representative Actors*, Frederick Warne and Co., Inscription, 1903.

Strachey, Lytton, *Characters and Commentaries*, Chatto and Windus, 1933.

Thraliana, Diary of Mrs Hester Lynch Thrale, Oxford University Press, 1951.

Toynbee, William, ed., *Macready's Diaries*, Chapman and Hall, 1912.

Trewin, J. C., *The Pomping Folk*, Dent, 1968.

Walpole, Horace, *Letters*, Richard Bentley and Son, 1840.

Wilkinson, Tate, *The Wandering Patentee*, 1795.